# A TREE OF POISON

## SILICON VALLEY MURDER BOOK 3

### VICTORIA KAZARIAN

*To Pete*
*For selflessly teaching me*
*to love games and Star Trek*

*I was angry with my friend;*
*I told my wrath, my wrath did end.*
*I was angry with my foe:*
*I told it not; my wrath did grow.*
*And I waterd it in fears,*
*Night and morning with my tears:*
*And I sunned it with smiles,*
*And with soft deceitful wiles.*
*And it grew both day and night.*
*Till it bore an apple bright.*
*And my foe beheld it shine,*
*And he knew that it was mine.*
*And into my garden stole,*
*When the night had veiled the pole*
*In the morning glad I see*
*My foe outstretched beneath the tree.*

*-William Blake*

# 1

---

*January 28*
*Five years ago*

Only bad things happen after midnight. Murders. Drunk drivers. Kids throwing up on your side of the bed.

The call came at 12:30 a.m. Because murder usually doesn't take place during business hours.

Detective James Ruiz rolled over and reached for his cell phone on the nightstand. Reyna was getting up early to go to the gym, so he immediately turned the ringer off. He pressed the phone close to his ear and heard dispatcher Kelly Arteaga's clipped, no-nonsense tone.

"Triple homicide on Folsom Road, Jimmy. Residents are Brent and Jennie Miller, and son Christopher. Robbery, possible home invasion. Neighbor heard gunshots and saw a car pulling away. McConaughy and Collins are at the scene."

Ruiz rubbed the sleep from his eyes. He was awake now. Murder cases didn't come along every day in upscale Monte Verde.

"I'll be there in twenty-five."

James Ruiz slipped out of the bed and took out his night clothes—slacks, a dark sweater, and a jacket. He'd been out to investigate a late-night robbery a year ago. Luckily, everything still fit— sort of, he thought, as he tugged his sweater down over his belly. He grabbed his kit, pulled his shoes out and headed out to the living room to put them on.

He was tying up his shoes when he heard a small voice from the hallway.

"Papa, where are you going?" Four-year-old Jacky wandered into the hall in his Captain America pajamas, his black hair tousled from sleep and sweat. He must have heard the phone ring. "It's still the nighttime."

Ruiz stood up and the boy ran to him.

This last year, Jacky had decided he was the favored parent. Ruiz didn't mind it, and, in fact, loved it. He'd always worried that his relationship with his own father doomed him to fail at parenthood. He wasn't sure where he ranked, but being Jacky's father came naturally to him.

"I've gotta go out and help some people in Monte Verde." He hugged his son. "You need to go back to bed, *mijo*."

"Is it dangerous?" The boy looked up at him skeptically. "Promise me you'll come back."

Ruiz looked at him, amused. "Is there a time when I didn't come back?"

The boy twisted up his face as he thought about this. "No."

Ruiz smiled and got up, turning the boy around to face the hall. "Then you can go back to bed and not worry about it."

Jacky was not convinced. He looked back at him, yawning. "What if there are bad guys? What if they have guns?"

The boy had a point. Who was to say the killers were gone? That they wouldn't come back?

It was what he faced, what every cop faced. You assessed the risk, took precautions, and dealt with whatever happened using your weapon, your training, and your experience. The only problem was, in his seventeen years in upscale Monte Verde's police department, he hadn't had much experience with homicide.

*Three victims. Parents and a son.* Ruiz felt a lump in his throat.

"If they have guns, I know what to do. And I've got McConaughy and Collins with me. They're a lot tougher than me."

He shot a glance at the living room clock. In the interest of time, he picked up Jacky and carried him back to his bed. He gave him a kiss and pulled the covers over him.

"I will be back in time to take you to school," Ruiz said with conviction. He hoped it was true.

Then he pulled on his jacket and headed out the front door, feeling the chill of the crisp, clear January night.

He made sure to lock all three locks.

AFTER SPEEDING on empty freeways from his house in Santa Clara to Monte Verde, Ruiz drove up into the hills, turning from Laurelwood Road onto Folsom, a quiet road with custom homes. This wasn't an area you ended up in unless you knew where you were going, which could have made the families in this area complacent about safety. He pulled his truck up in front of the Miller's sprawling one story.

The white wood and stucco house sat on a plot with a good amount of land, an acre he judged—as much as a city kid like him could judge acreage. The house's backyard was sloped, part of the hillside, which ended up in a forest that went on for a while. There were houses on either side of the Millers, but they were far apart, all on large lots, unlike the tract homes farther down the hill on Folsom. Tall fir trees that had likely been there before the houses were built towered over these newcomers and made the area look more rural than it was.

Tonight, a chill wind rustled in this cul-de-sac of Folsom, and you had the feeling that you were nearing the end of civilization, your back up against the wilderness.

A place like this, anyone would think, would be safe from the terrors of crime.

There was a sign for a security company stuck in front of the juniper bushes next to the front door. Ruiz wondered how likely it would be that the Millers had a working system. They could have relied on the sign to shoo away any amateurish intruders. But those would be the only intruders it would scare off. If this was a home invasion, the intruders had probably watched the house over time, learning the Millers' routine and figuring out what kind of security system they were dealing with. If there wasn't one, this house was a prime target.

The door was open, so Ruiz went inside. At first, there were no signs that three people had died here. The front entry way was painted a soothing color of light brown and was lined with framed prints and an antique-looking mirror. All tasteful and elegant, something Reyna would approve of. It looked like something from her home décor magazines.

He saw the living room beyond, tidy, with expensive furniture and a colorful Persian rug. As he got closer, he began to see the signs—a large, darkened rectangle on the wall where a painting had hung, hooks still in place. Cables hanging down from a hole in the wall where a big screen TV had been. Shelves in sleek wood cabinets empty. Framed family photos and a glass vase lay on the floor, not judged worthy of stealing.

He took a moment to slip on gloves and called out. "Ruiz here."

His voice echoed off the walls.

In a few minutes, McConaughy appeared in the doorway, with a look on his face he'd never seen before. The normally smiling patrol officer's face was pinched and white.

"The door was unlocked when we got here," the officer said hoarsely. "There are some footprints in the hallway, so watch your step. We're back in the bedrooms. With the deceased."

Ruiz avoided stepping on the footprints, which looked like the tread of athletic shoes, edged with blood.

"The adults looked like they tried to fight off their assailants. The teenager's by the door of his room, like he'd gotten up to see what the commotion was about."

Ruiz had been visualizing someone Jacky's age. It was still horrific and shouldn't have made a difference, but now that he knew the kid was older, he was overcome with relief. His mind could stop visualizing Jacky in the kid's place.

Ruiz followed McConaughy back to the bedrooms.

First the teenager's—There was a hand drawn sign on his door: *Christopher's Room – Trekkies only.*

The young man lay on his side, his blue eyes staring blankly out the door. His t-shirt was soaked with blood. The intruders had shot to kill, hitting his chest. He lay in a pool of dark blood.

McConaughy connected with Ruiz's eyes.

"Nail this one, Jimmy." The older cop's face tensed up as he looked down at the boy. "Jesus. I want to see these guys go down."

Ruiz looked down at the kid's fresh face, with a trace of blond fuzz under his nose—the beginnings of a mustache. A kid with his life ahead of him. Judging by the neat desk in the kid's room, stacked with textbooks, Christopher Miller had been a smart kid. Maybe bound for medical or law school. Or maybe he'd be a software programmer, like so many in the valley.

It wasn't like Ruiz had never seen this type of violence. It was more common in East San Jose where he'd grown up than in Monte Verde. He'd become accustomed to the lack of violent crime in the town he'd worked in for eighteen years.

But once he had a wife and a child, he'd never look at domestic crime scenes the same way.

He followed McConaughy across the hall to the largest master bedroom he'd ever seen. There was a king-sized bed, dressers and two armoires, and what looked like a walk-in closet. A big easy chair by the window to relax in. And lots of white carpet over the open space.

Officer Collins was in the room with the crime scene photographer, who was taking shots of various angles in the room.

The two of them blocked Ruiz's view, which was fine for now. Ruiz took out his tablet and began taking notes.

"We found no signs of forced entry." McConaughy turned to him, his eyes bloodshot. "There was a camera mounted inside, over the front door, but it's been smashed.

Looks like large items, mostly electronics, were taken. The big screen, probably desktop computers in the study, the kid's bedroom and in here, judging by the dust patterns on the desks."

Collins, a small wiry officer, left the photographer to do his thing and approached Ruiz.

Ruiz now saw the two bodies. The couple looked like they'd been stopped, mid-action. A bloody baseball bat lay on the floor a few feet from the woman, who was sprawled alongside the bed, blood covering her torso. Her hand lay stretched out, as if she'd been reaching up to catch a fly ball.

The man was crumpled over, his back against the side of the dresser as if he'd slid down it. His head slumped over his chest. Only after bending down did Ruiz see, with a wave of revulsion, the man had been shot in the face. Ruiz suddenly felt nausea rise in his stomach, roiling with the large helpings of Filipino food he'd eaten for dinner.

"There's a small handgun on his left. A .38 Special. Looks like he didn't get a chance to shoot it." There was a twitch in Collins' eye that Ruiz hadn't noticed before. "I'm surprised the assailants didn't take it."

Ruiz looked at the trail of blood leading a few feet beyond the baseball bat. "The woman may have landed a hit. This could be her blood, or it could be the assailant's." He wrote down a note for the crime scene team and hoped they'd be here soon.

Ruiz also noted what looked like another set of footprints, but these looked different. No tread. He snapped a photo on his phone. If this was true, there were at least two assailants.

He wanted to know how they had gotten in.

After he did a walk-through of the house, checking doors, Ruiz concluded that the assailants had either come in through the garage, and entered the main part of the house through the kitchen—or had followed someone in the front door. In either case, if Jennie and Brent Miller had been in bed, and it looked like they were, they had been in the back, far corner of the house. They wouldn't have heard someone entering through the front door or the garage.

He opened the door to the garage and flipped on the light next to the door. There was a BMW inside, a sleek, black 6 series. Ruiz stopped just a second or two to give it a longing look, then headed around it to the garage door. He didn't notice anything unusual about it, so he moved on to the side door, which looked like it led out to the house's side yard. It was locked.

If the assailants had wanted to get in badly enough, they would have had a dozen ways at their disposal to do so. But there would be signs of forced entry, and he didn't see any.

By the time he'd gotten back inside, the medical examiner was working on Mrs. Miller. Ruiz had seen Dr. Santosh Aggarwal before at a couple of vehicular fatalities on Foothill Expressway. He was businesslike and quick but willing to answer questions on what he was seeing.

"It looks like she fought back. Any signs of that? Skin under the fingernails?" Ruiz asked as the doctor examined the woman.

"It doesn't look like it." The doctor examined the woman's hands and shook his head. He looked at the bat lying a couple feet away from the woman. "I don't think she got close enough before he shot. Can't bring a baseball bat to a gunfight."

"The blood on the bat. We'll test to see if it's hers," Ruiz said, almost to himself. She was dead, so was her husband and son. For some reason, he wanted to know that the woman had tried to fight back. That she'd managed to inflict a wound on her killer and hadn't accepted her fate so easily.

Dr. Aggarwal looked up and tilted his head. "Of course. Might be splatter. I suppose she could have hit him."

Within an hour, the three bodies were taken away. Ruiz stayed as the crime scene team went over the bedrooms and the entry points, doing a sweep for fingerprints, blood and any physical evidence left by the assailants.

As he walked through the house carefully, looking for anything he might have missed, Ruiz jotted down details or methods that might pin down the people who did this. Often thieves had their MO, telltale signs for their hits.

Home invasions, by anyone other than amateurs, were often the work of gangs, organized groups who targeted areas where people made a lot of money. These groups spent time monitoring their targets and often practiced for their hits. They were looking for big ticket items to sell. What was unusual with the Millers' case was that three people had been killed in the process. Though home invasions were on the rise, people weren't usually killed.

The Millers were a hindrance, of no value to the thieves. Their lives were snuffed out as easily as he'd slap a mosquito on his arm.

As he imagined the quiet night at the Millers, hours before the invasion began, he pictured the family at dinner: the parents talking about their days at work as they ate, Mr. Miller cracking a lame joke that made the son roll his eyes. Maybe they'd talked about a camping trip they were planning for the summer. The teenaged son downed his food quickly, eager to finish his homework so he could play video games.

As soon as he got to the station the next morning, Ruiz would begin his research. He'd search state databases for invasions. He'd call the detectives on the cases, looking for any details that might be a match.

He would find the killers and do everything to build his case—documenting everything to the letter, his paperwork and reports perfect, so that when these guys were arrested, there would be no doubt of a conviction.

One week went by without a match. After interviewing friends of the Millers, Ruiz learned that Christopher had been at a friend's house playing Dungeons and Dragons that night. He'd come home at 11:30 p.m. The killers had probably followed him right in.

To Ruiz's disappointment, tests on the bat only showed Jennie Miller's blood. Two months passed with a few leads that didn't pan out, and Sergeant Dave Schallert told Ruiz he needed to move on. After one year, the case slipped into the cold case files.

But that night at the Millers stayed with Ruiz. It was a year before the images stuck on repeat in his head went away.

After a couple of years, the Miller home invasion became a local legend, something kids used to scare themselves with when they rode their bikes by the house. On the second anniversary of the murders, Ruiz drove up Folsom Road. He saw a Pending Sale sign in the front yard. But even after the sale, the house stood empty for a year, its lawn repossessed by the wilderness around it. Weeds and overgrown succulent plants grew untended on either side of the front walkway.

One evening after work, Ruiz took a turn onto Folsom and drove to the end of the street, just to see the place again. To his surprise, the Miller house had been completely demolished.

He shouldn't have been surprised—lots were expensive

in this area and a home where three people were brutally murdered wasn't going to do well on the housing market. Somebody'd bought the lot, planning to rebuild.

The coastal redwood trees surrounding the house looked naked and exposed around the ruins. The forest behind looked bigger, darker and deeper now; as if the wilderness was pounding its chest. It had triumphed over civilization.

*You humans, you come, go, and kill each other. We were here before you, and we will be here after you.*

Bulldozers were parked around the lot, abandoned like toys in a kid's sandbox. Heaps of concrete, rebar, dry wall, and white siding lay where a house had been.

Construction work was done for the day, so Ruiz parked and got out to walk the property.

This had been a home.

As he walked around the lot, he couldn't get away from that idea. The Millers had made a life here, worked, eaten, played, and slept here.

Now it was gone.

Two months later, the house was finished. It was huge and had a fake Mediterranean look to it—pink stucco, with balconies and elaborate wrought iron decorations. A McMansion.

When Ruiz drove by, he automatically replaced it with the old house in his mind—the way it must have been in the days before the invasion. Planted on the hillside, surrounded by the towering stand of fir trees in the dark, hilly reaches of Folsom Road.

It was the last time he'd seen the quiet town of Monte Verde as a safe place.

## 2

*February 20*
*Current day*

Detective Dani Grasso had moved into her boyfriend Tom Weber's house in stages.

First, her toothbrush and toiletries. She'd need them if she was spending the night. Then as she ended up staying through the week, it made sense to buy a small dresser to keep a few changes of clothes at Tom's. But eventually the reality of a five-minute commute to Monte Verde PD made the decision for her.

She boxed up her clothes and outerwear, packed up her PlayStation and games she played regularly, and took them to Tom's. She got rid of her landline. The only person who'd called her on it was her grandfather, Giovanni Grasso, founder of Grasso's Fine Foods, and she wasn't sure how she felt about him now.

With that, she'd become a *de facto* resident of Monte Verde, the town she worked in.

The condo in Cupertino near Apple Headquarters was still hers. Her grandfather had bought it for her as a college graduation present. And when family wanted to visit, she met them there—and she acted like she was there every day.

She hated being dishonest. Her family, with their impossible expectations, left her with no choice.

She hadn't even told her parents or any of her family that she had...a *boyfriend*. The word sounded strange, full of middle school drama. And a little ridiculous when she applied it to the 46-year-old man she was seeing.

Her parents had been bugging her to pair up since high school. *Seeing anybody? Have you met anyone yet? Maybe if you didn't spend all your time playing games, Daniela.*

She now had a boyfriend who played games with her. So, *score!*

Tom was chill, a matter-of-fact man who was practically drama-free. Some nights they fell asleep intertwined on the couch, after hard days at work and an intense video game campaign.

When she'd taken the detective position at Monte Verde PD, her family first responded with outrage. It was assumed that she'd take a job at Grasso's Fine Foods after graduation. The family business.

Like her aunt Lidia and uncle Stefano. Her father. Her brothers, Alex and Anthony. All worked in management at GFF headquarters—its flagship store in Saratoga—or one of the chain's five Bay Area stores.

But that day in her grandfather's office, on the day that should have been her first day in the family business, she'd said no.

She'd always dreamed of being a detective.

Giovanni Grasso—or Unnon, as she called her Neapolitan grandfather—was furious.

Unnon eventually called her and told her he'd accepted her decision. He assured her that he'd talk to her dad and tell him he was okay with her new career.

He never did.

Of course, if he did, it would probably start an exodus of family members also realizing *they* had other career options.

For almost a year, Dani held her ground, throwing herself into the job she'd always wanted, mentored by Detective Jimmy Ruiz. She didn't see or hear much from her tight-knit family.

Now that things were cautiously starting to improve, she was reluctant to tell them she had a boyfriend. A boyfriend who was only six years younger than her parents. And Tom was neither Catholic nor Italian.

They'd met on last year's big case, the murder of his boss, Infinitas CEO Rosalind Mabrey. During the investigation, Tom had been hospitalized after the crash of his Corvette.

He was now working remotely in his Monte Verde home as Infinitas Director of Operations, as his mangled leg healed.

From the moment she'd met him during the interviews for the Mabrey case, something about Tom had gently tugged at her. She'd gone out of her way to visit him in the hospital, then as he recovered from his injury at home, he'd shyly invited her over and they'd started having video game dates. In contrast to her family relationships, her time with Tom felt natural. Effortless. There was no drama. Most of the time she felt layers of stress lift off her when she was with him.

So far, she hadn't had to tell her family anything.

Her job and relationship kept her busy, and she wasn't often down in Saratoga near her family anyway. Unnon had family get-togethers at his home every few months. She went by herself, pigged out on tables of Italian food and wine, and talked family business and (sparingly) the business of detective work. She was able to live her new life *and* keep her family at a safe distance. It was working out so far.

Maybe she could keep her relationship a secret a little longer.

Then one day at the station while she sat finishing up some paperwork, she received a series of texts that sent a chill down her spine. Anthony's face, from a leering selfie he'd taken as a teenager, came up as the contact.

She could almost hear his voice speaking the words:

YOU HAVE BEEN SEEN. BRING HIM TO
THE NEXT FAMILY DINNER.

OR WE'LL TELL EVERYBODY, FUCKING
EVERYBODY,

FUCK ALL

**3**

———

"Hey, Ruiz. Got a minute?"

Ruiz typically avoided Frank Ladera at all costs. But now the older detective stood in front of Ruiz's desk, a grin on his face and a flyer in his hand.

Last year, Ladera had helped Ruiz when he desperately needed it, taking him aside and giving him advice on navigating the divorce process.

It had practically killed Ruiz to ask for it, but Ladera had given it, with kindness and even some wisdom, gained from his messy split with his wife the year before. So far Ruiz hadn't needed to use the advice.

Ruiz managed a smile. "Sure, Frank. What's up?"

"We're having a party for my birthday. At Garcia's. This Friday night in the backroom. Free burritos for everyone. You in?"

Frank, as usual, had to round up attendees for his own birthday party, and he was bribing people to come. Ruiz didn't want to go, but Frank considered him a friend.

The right thing to do was to say yes, and then try to rope in other fun people to come along, so the party was bearable. He'd spent too many nights watching Niners games at Frank's empty one-bedroom apartment. The detective was terrified of being alone.

He could use Reyna as an excuse. That she wanted him home. She was going out with the work ladies, and he needed to stay home with Jacky.

But, this morning he had feelings of goodwill welling up inside him. Their most recent marriage counseling session hadn't been as intense as he'd expected. He'd only been in the hot seat once; he was feeling generous.

"Sure, Frank. Let's do this." He smiled up at the man, whose face lit up.

"That's great. Great, Jimmy," he responded with glee.

A bounce in his step, Ladera moved on to the next desk and repeated his pitch.

At the coffee station, Ruiz ran into Grasso, who was pouring coffee into her oversized mug. She looked unhappy —or tired, which would explain the coffee.

"Hey, sunshine." He raised his mug and tapped hers when she'd filled it. "How's your morning so far?

Grasso scowled. "Fucking awful."

She'd been swearing a lot lately, which was something new for Grasso, who'd come onto the force as a sweet and sheltered academy graduate—a good Catholic girl. It was like hearing profanity pour out of the mouth of a young kid. It would take him a while to get used to it.

He waved his mug in the direction of the conference room. "I'm waiting to get in with Schallert. He's got somebody in there right now. Wanna talk?"

Grasso nodded reluctantly, looking distracted. Ruiz was curious as to what this was about. Trouble with Tom? The two of them had seemed crazy for each other last time Tom came by the station to pick Grasso up. They'd exchanged squishy looks so often that it had been embarrassing to be in the room with them. Ruiz could be reading this wrong today—it might not be Tom at all. She could be dealing with a setback on the domestic case she was working.

He pulled out a chair and took a seat at the long table. Grasso set her mug down on the table and sat down across from him.

She sat back in her seat, her face grim and her eyes red rimmed.

"I'm being blackmailed."

Ruiz's eyes widened as adrenaline surged through his body.

*What the hell?* He tried to process what she'd just said. Then it came to him.

"Okay. This is about your family."

She nodded and took a big gulp from her mug. "One of my brothers saw me and Tom out somewhere. Apparently, we were engaging in PDA. It's not like we even do that very often. We might have been holding hands. A peck on the cheek. That kind of thing."

Ruiz tried to keep a straight face. Those were tame public displays of affection. "I don't get it. Where does the blackmailing come in?"

"Anthony texted me that if I don't bring 'the new boyfriend' to the next extended family get-together at my grandfather's, he's going to tell everyone about Tom."

Ruiz shrugged. "He's probably joking. Brothers do that. Call his bluff."

Grasso gave him a piercing look, the likes of which he'd never seen from her.

"Jimmy, you don't understand. This is *my family*." She turned her round dark eyes on him. "They didn't speak to me for almost a year when I told them I wasn't going to work at Grasso's Fine Foods. These people mean business."

Ruiz shrugged. What was he missing here? This didn't seem like a big deal, though from what Grasso shared with him, her parents had strict ideas about what she should be doing with her life and who she should be doing it with.

"Tom's a good guy." Ruiz studied her face, trying to pinpoint the source of her frustration. "I don't see why anyone would have a problem with him."

"Right? But he's more than twenty years older than me. And he's not Catholic." She rubbed her eyes. "Tom doesn't know how my family works. He's nice—and he's *normal*. I don't want to expose him to their shit."

Two swears in five minutes.

Ruiz leaned in across the table. The first thing that came to mind was a football analogy, but he got the feeling that wasn't something Grasso would relate to, and he pulled back. Marriage counseling was helping him with more things than just his marriage.

"Don't let 'em know you're scared, Dani. Go on the offensive. Come up with something Anthony and Alex won't expect."

Grasso leaned on her arm and looked across the table at him. Her eyes brightened a little.

"Maybe I could bring Tom to meet my grandfather. Just us," she said, as if she were testing out the idea. "If he approves of Tom, they might back off. And everyone would be okay with it." She sat back and let out a loud sigh. "But then, I'm still waiting for Unnon to tell my dad he's okay with me working *here*."

"You think that'll work?" Grasso wasn't on great terms with her grandfather, though from what Grasso said, the old man respected her more than her brothers.

"When it comes down to it, I need to introduce Tom to my family. But I don't want to do it my brother's way. I thought I could keep those two parts of my life separate, but it looks like I can't."

Grasso's voice had returned to its normal level of confidence, and he felt relieved.

"Tom's smart. He's got a lot of money and he's a likeable guy. Your parents should be happy." Through the window in the door, Ruiz saw Schallert come out of his office. Ruiz stood up. "But you know your family much better than I do. They might get upset that he's older. Or not a good Italian boy—I mean uh, *man*. But look—you were cut off from them for a year and you survived."

"Yeah, thanks for being so comforting, Jimmy," Grasso smirked at him as she stood up. "But you're right. I can't let Alex and Anthony get to me. They're trying to pull the same things they did to terrorize me when I was little. Fuck that."

It had been two years since Grasso had been hired. She'd seemed very young—and he'd suspected her hire as a detective had been fast-tracked by the Grasso name. The first step toward becoming a detective was normally working two to five years on patrol. Not to say she wasn't a qualified candidate. She'd graduated from San Jose State with a criminal justice degree and had gone straight into the academy that summer.

He'd remembered her on her first day, off-the-charts enthusiastic and looking about fourteen years old. At first her perkiness and optimism had given him a headache. She'd worked hard, had taken on anything, and had grown in confidence since that first day. She'd used her intuition and perseverance to close the Mabrey case, when Ruiz had been struggling to stay focused, with the prospect of Reyna leaving him.

She'd come on the force as an innocent, a good Catholic girl with a fierce passion for doing what was right. For seeing justice done.

He even remembered her praying to St. Jude, the saint of lost causes, for his marriage. Who knows. With the way things were going with Reyna, it might have worked.

Now he looked at her almost as a father would—and saw that she was growing up fast. He suspected she was living with Tom Weber here in Monte Verde, though he wasn't ready to ask, and she probably wasn't going to tell him.

And now, the swearing. Surrounded by mostly men in the station, she could be doing it to fit in, to act tough. He swore all the time, but it was a shock for it to be coming out of *her* mouth.

As they went out the door together and Ruiz headed for Schallert's office, he told himself Dani Grasso was, just like his marriage, a work in process.

I⊤ WAS cold and windy outside that evening, and a light rain had started to fall.

Tom ordered Indian food delivery for dinner. He'd had a series of budget meetings online all day and was wiped out from a physical therapy session on his leg. They ate in the living room so he could half sit, half lay in the recliner with his leg elevated.

"How exactly—where would we meet your grandfather?" Tom asked cautiously. Tom dipped his garlic naan in raita sauce and pulled off a big bite with his teeth. "How would this work?"

He was a little nervous, Grasso could see. It made her

angry that she'd been pushed into doing something like this. But she couldn't keep her relationship secret forever. And of all her family, 84-year-old Giovanni Grasso would behave himself the best. He may or may not approve of Tom, but he'd be a gracious host and with just him, there would be no complications from her brothers and father.

"We'd go to his house in Saratoga. His chef, Milvia, will prepare a meal for us—usually four courses. It'll be the most delicious food you've ever eaten. Then we drink wine —really, really good wine from his cellar, decades old—and talk. He can be very charming. He'll ask about your work and where you're from. Be prepared for him to talk about Naples and how bad the supply chain is right now."

Tom was quiet for a while. "This sounds like a big deal for your family, Dani. Is this some kind of test?"

Grasso had a forkful of her butter chicken. She didn't know what to say to that. Because it was a test. He hadn't met any of her family. This would be the first. But if he didn't pass, she told herself it would make no difference to her. She was tired of them trying to control her choices.

"My brother spotted us downtown and threatened to tell everybody in the family we're seeing each other. He's being annoying about it, but maybe it makes sense for you to start meeting them." Suddenly, she was hit by the uneasy feeling that this signaled a step up in their relationship. By asking him to meet the family, she was sealing a commitment between them.

A commitment she wasn't sure she was ready for. Marriage. Oh, God, maybe kids. She was twenty-five. It's not like she didn't care for Tom. Maybe she even loved him. But those things seemed overwhelming, and she shouldn't have to think about them for a long, long time.

"It makes sense to meet them." Tom wiped his lips with

a napkin and took a chug of Indian lager. "I'm up for it. Let me know what night works. It's budgeting time at Infinitas, and I have meetings through the weekend. Weekday evenings for the next two weeks should be okay. Just give me some advance notice."

She'd call Unnon tomorrow and set something up.

There, she'd settled it. She thought she'd feel less anxious once she'd talked to Tom about it, but now she felt worse. How was he interpreting this? Did this mean something to Tom—something she didn't intend?

Anthony had put her in a difficult situation, and she'd been furious. She tried to preempt him but wasn't sure it would work and didn't feel much better now.

Maybe he'd won anyway.

SHE AND TOM played *Sands of Illustra*, a role-playing adventure game, until 11 p.m. After a few failed attempts they worked together to beat a Megaworm boss. They laughed when a non-player character, an orange, tentacled mutant with a cowboy hat, drawled its repeated phrase in a nasal voice:

*We shall return to fight as partners ere the suns of Azir rise.*

"I'm pretty sure the suns of Azir have risen fifty times by now. And he keeps saying that. We're still not beating this guy," Grasso groaned.

"We can do this. C'mon, Dani," Tom planted a kiss on her cheek, as they respawned and headed back to the same area of the game.

They died several times and after three respawns they finally did it, with a coordinated attack—Tom coming in close in the megaworm's shadow, while she stood at a distance and shot fiery arrows.

They high-fived each other, then in minutes Tom was snoring. His head lay in her lap, and soon she leaned back against the stack of pillows and dozed off.

Then the call came on her cell phone. She fumbled for her phone on the end table.

Ruiz.

His voice sounded choked. Distant.

"There's been a home invasion in the hills. 19225 Maldonado. Cross street is Folsom. McConaughy and Rogers are there. I'm sure you're closer. Meet you there in 25 minutes."

There was a pause for a few seconds. Then she heard Ruiz's hoarse voice.

"There's a body."

## 4

————

Ruiz's words set off a surge of adrenaline. She was awake now.

*A body.*

She gently slid her leg out from under Tom's head and replaced it with a pillow.

She still needed to get rid of her grogginess. She and Tom had finished off a bottle of pinot noir after dinner.

"What is it?" Tom opened his eyes and blinked. His voice was husky and full of sleep.

"A home invasion. Not far from here."

"Holy shit." Tom sat up suddenly.

His face had an expression of grave concern, yet a cowlick of grey-brown hair stood up on his head in a comical way. Like the crest of a bird. She wanted to laugh. She wanted to lay back down next to him.

But more than that, she wanted to be out in the night, plunged into a new case.

"Ruiz said there was a home invasion a few years before I joined the force. You lived here, so you must remember it. I'm surprised it doesn't happen more often here."

"The Millers." Tom said, in a whisper. "I remember. Dani, be careful."

If she wanted to be lazy about it, she was already dressed since they'd fallen asleep in their clothes. Choosing to look professional, she went upstairs to her dresser in Tom's closet and changed. Black slacks, clean white wool sweater. She pulled her black blazer off the hanger.

She looked out Tom's front window and saw the porch light shining on a walkway slick from the rain. Boots would be wise. After slipping her boots on, she went downstairs to the couch and kissed Tom's scruffy face.

Dani pulled on her jacket. "It'll be fine. The perpetrators are gone. Patrol officers will be there, and the medical examiner for the body—"

"Murder." A shadow of fear crossed his face. "Jesus."

He rubbed his eyes and lay back down on the couch, sinking into the pile of throw pillows.

From somewhere in the pillow nest, she heard something muffled. It might have been *love you*.

She headed downstairs to her car in the garage.

DANI BACKED her Mini Cooper out of Tom's garage and tapped the remote to close the door.

The night was overcast, and the full moon behind the clouds touched them with an eerie glow.

The cold, sharp air on her skin was stripping away her grogginess. She was alert now.

From Tom's home on Laurelwood Road, she drove down Folsom and turned onto Maldonado, a short, curved street ending in a cul-de-sac. The houses here were large and far apart. Sprawling custom homes with three-car garages, and glass windows from floor to ceiling, some with views of the forested hills, some with glimpses of the bay and valley below—which looked their best when farther away.

As they approached the hills, Monte Verde's streets curved, dictated by the topography. Folsom Road was long and straight until it curved around the slopes of the wooded hills that led into the Santa Cruz Mountains.

Maldonado Road branched off from Folsom. The road was named for a local family who built there sixty years ago when the valley below was known more for its fruit orchards than its technology.

Both the end of Folsom and the end of Maldonado backed up against the steep hills, a forested area that felt like the beginning of the wilderness. People lived there for many reasons: privacy, safety, and a natural quiet, removed from the busy Silicon Valley below.

Beyond the houses at the end of the street fir and redwood trees stood like a dark wall. She heard a rustle in the trees, as if something was pushing its way through them.

She pulled up in front of the large house, a two-story with a yard that looked appealing and professionally landscaped. White camelias bushes bloomed across the front of the house, and a picturesque Japanese maple tree arched next to the walkway, its delicate leaves spinning like tiny hands in the wind.

Lights blazed in the windows of the home, making it stand out among the darkened houses spread out on the short street. Two patrol cars sat on the street in front of the house.

The door was ajar, light shining inside, so she entered. "Hey, Andy."

She nodded at Andrew Rogers, who was hired as a patrol officer not long before she came on the force. He was a former marine with the same buzzed haircut he probably had in the service, a sharp nose and close-set blue eyes.

"You got here fast, Grasso."

"Ruiz is on his way." She started to take in the house as she waited in the hallway. The door looked unscathed. She wondered if the killer or killers had been let in—or had used another entrance.

"As you go through the house, you'll see. Obvious things taken, computers, a nice theatre-style big screen TV ripped out of the wall. The office upstairs is ransacked, papers everywhere."

"The guy's in the bedroom. He was shot in bed. Just to warn you, it's not pretty—"

Dani bristled. "I can handle it," she snapped at him, which made the officer blink in surprise. In the Mabrey case last year, she'd seen her first dead body and had promptly hurled her breakfast. She was sure that story made the rounds at the station. She was still sensitive about it.

"Okay, Andy, give me the deets." She flashed him a smile to make up for her brusqueness. "Got an ID on him?"

"Derrick Winslow, according to the driver's license in his wallet. I googled the guy. He's an entrepreneur—helps start tech companies in the valley. Older guy. 52, divorced, one kid." Her parents' age.

"Let's go see him." Grasso said, taking out her tablet and a pair of gloves.

Rogers led the way up the stairs, planks of concrete mounted onto an iron rail, to give the illusion that they were floating. As they climbed, Grasso looked out over the great room to her left.

Nothing much looked disturbed in the room, but she did see the mount and cables for the very large, big screen TV that had been taken. Something had been removed from the wall—a painting or some sort of wall hanging. The empty space where it had hung was a brighter color than the wall around it.

Grasso jotted down her observations. If the idea was to come up with an MO for this invasion, to match with other cases by the same gang or assailants, she wanted to have info ready.

"Here's the office." Rogers waved her into a large, spacious room, with a window looking out over the forest behind the house. During the day, it must be a beautiful view. Now it looked dark and spooky. With only faint light in the backyard, it was hard to see much, though a vague shuffling movement in the branches that made it look like some ghostly presence was moving the darkened trees.

Papers littered the floor of the office. Drawers were left hanging open, in the large natural wood desk, and in the filing cabinets. There was a large narrow safe, and it was open. It didn't look like any organized search to Grasso. Other than the safe, it looked like someone had made a mess to prove a point. Why would the same people who stole a big screen TV be after something in Derrick Winslow's papers? Unless they were looking for something specific hidden in the drawers. Something they knew was there. Maybe this hadn't been a random invasion.

Officer McConaughy came out in the hall, finishing up a call on his radio.

"Dr. Aggarwal the ME is on his way. He'll be here in about 15. You wanna come in and see the victim?"

As Grasso prepared to answer, there was a noise downstairs, then steps reverberating on the concrete stairs.

"Ruiz here." She heard his familiar voice in the stairwell and felt a sudden sense of calm. She paused at the top of the stairs.

Jimmy Ruiz looked wide awake. As if he hadn't polished off a bottle of wine the night before.

"Night roadwork on 101. Sorry for the delay." Ruiz nodded at McConaughy and Rogers. "Let's take a look at the guy."

The three of them filed into the bedroom. Grasso saw the body in the bed, blood soaking the pillow and bedclothes, and she was okay. Then, she and Ruiz walked around the bed to examine the scene. At first, she had a hard time figuring out what she was seeing. Ruiz standing next to her became so rigid that she could feel it.

"His face—" Her voice came out so weak she didn't recognize it.

Derrick Winslow had been shot in the face. From a close range. What was there now was unrecognizable as human.

Ruiz had his tablet out and was taking notes. He didn't talk for several minutes. He walked around the bed looking over the room. Then he walked out down the hall. She didn't want to stay in the bedroom either, so she followed him.

He was in the office, looking at the papers on the floor and the drawers pulled out. He rubbed his face and stood for a while. Then he walked out into the hall, pacing back and forth. Grasso knew this meant two things: 1) Ruiz was thinking, and 2) he was pissed off.

He nodded. "Let's check all the entrances."

They made their way down the stairs. After searching the downstairs, they spotted the garage-to-living room entrance and went out to check the garage door and a side door to the backyard.

Locked and unscathed.

They spotted double doors to the backyard, which were intact and locked. They reminded Grasso of Tom's French doors, which opened onto the deck and a beautiful view. Then they found another door from a downstairs bedroom that led to a deck in the backyard. Locked. No signs that it had been forced open.

"How did they get in?"

Ruiz shook his head. "It's possible that someone in the house let them in—or they followed someone in. That's what happened with the Millers. They followed Christopher Miller in when he got home late."

"But it looked like Derrick Winslow had gone to bed."

"Maybe he had an overnight visitor. It doesn't look like the alarm had been set."

"What are you thinking?" Grasso searched Ruiz's face. Something had upset him. Of course, the sight of Winslow was disturbing. She was surprised she hadn't had a worse reaction, given her history. Maybe, at this hour, the shock of what she'd seen hadn't registered yet.

"*Déjà vu.* That's what I'm thinking." He was typing on his tablet with his usual hunt and peck method. She saw his screen: 1. *Shot in face; 2. Same items taken; 3. Office ransacked. 4. No sign of forced entry.*

Below that he'd written: *Victim in bed. Maybe asleep when shot.*

At 12:15, they went back upstairs. Dr. Aggarwal was in the bedroom examining Winslow.

"Jimmy, good to see you again." Ruiz had last seen the examiner a year ago at a traffic fatality in downtown Monte Verde. The man looked up to flash a smile at Ruiz. "How old's your boy now?"

"He's nine now. Fourth grade. Santosh, I'd like you to meet my partner, Detective Dani Grasso."

Grasso gave the examiner an abrupt nod, thinking it was

weird for Ruiz to be talking about his young son in this place of death.

"Dr. Aggarwal," she asked the examiner. "Would you know if the victim was awake when he was shot?"

"I can't know that for sure, detective." The examiner said. "Judging by his position and the pooling of the blood, he was shot here in the bed."

"Any similarities between his injuries and Brent Miller's?" Ruiz asked.

"Just that Winslow was shot in the face, like Mr. Miller." Aggarwal raised his eyebrows. "Similar injuries just because of the weapon and the range at which it was shot. We may know more with the autopsy."

McConaughy poked his head in the door. "Just to let you know, Ruiz. On our initial search, we didn't find a gun."

Ruiz nodded. "We'll go through again and see what we can find."

After another search of the house, Ruiz and Grasso sat in Ruiz's truck to conference.

"Winslow's house is three blocks from the Millers'." Ruiz zipped up his jacket and rubbed his hands. They'd had a reprieve from the cold inside.

"I was on the scene with patrol a half hour after the Millers were killed." Ruiz continued, opening the door of the truck a crack since they were fogging up the windows. He looked out the windshield, his face clouded. "It was the worst crime scene I've seen in Monte Verde."

"Anyone arrested?"

"We tried to make a connection with other home invasion robberies but never found a match."

"I'll get right on this in the morning." Grasso said. "We can check the database. These invasions aren't usually isolated incidents, right?"

Ruiz beat his fingers on his steering wheel. "Monte Verde is an attractive target for people who do this, and there are a lot of upscale homes in this part of the Bay Area. I hope to hell we don't see any more of these. I'll have Tyler in PR put a bulletin out, warning people to lock up and set their alarms. And be on the lookout for suspicious cars in their neighborhoods."

Ruiz turned to Grasso with a curious look.

"Rogers and McConaughy told me you got here in record time tonight."

Grasso's face was deadpan. "I drive fast."

"Your boyfriend has a nice house." Ruiz finally cracked a smile. "If I could live in a place like that, I would, too."

Dani drove back to Tom's, feeling wired and awake at 2 a.m. She went through the house and made sure every door was locked. She set the alarm downstairs.

Tom had gone upstairs to bed, and as she wandered through the downstairs, she suddenly felt a pang of loneliness and desolation.

She was tempted to blow it off by playing a video game, but she knew herself. If she started in on a game, she'd never get to bed. She'd miss her morning run at Rancho San Antonio, and she'd be cranky and out of sorts once she got to the station.

It was probably too late to wake Tom up for sex, though it was what she wanted.

As Tom snored softly on his side, she stripped down and slipped under the covers. She pressed her body against his warm back.

"You're back. You're okay." He turned to face her. His sleepy voice was raspy and very sexy.

He rolled over and kissed her lips, then moved down and kissed her breasts. Soon he was touching her in all the right places. When he slipped into her, hard and deep, everything she'd seen tonight faded to the background. She wanted to moan, to scream, and, strangely, to giggle. She was on a swing, soaring high, then higher still than she thought possible.

She wanted to stop it. She could not control this. Finally, she had no choice but to give into it, till she lay, laughing inside as he pressed into her one last time.

She was glad she hadn't settled for the video game.

**5**

———

The entryway was dark and silent when Ruiz came in the front door of his house.

A tidy row of shoes lined up inside the door. The dishwasher hummed. All surfaces shone, from the coffee table in the living room to the kitchen counters. No clutter.

Everything from the day put back in place, so the next day could start from a place of order and neatness.

After their son Jacky, it was the best thing Reyna had given him.

He hadn't grown up in a house like this. He, his mother, and his little brother Mateo had lived in a series of apartments in east San Jose, after his father had disappeared from their lives. Lupe Maria Ruiz had tried, but after a full day of cleaning houses for people in wealthy Saratoga and Los Gatos, she didn't have energy left to clean her own. Dirty dishes lay stacked on the counter and trash bins overflowed. Ruiz did what he could to pitch in between school, work, and football, but he'd never invited his friends over.

Ruiz gulped down a glass of water in the kitchen, then considered trying to figure out where Reyna had hidden the chips. He'd enjoyed the hunt, and it used to be his go-to stress relief to pull out the bag and crunch on something salty. Last year, he'd made an adult decision: It wasn't good for him, and he didn't need it. Whether or not he stayed with Reyna through the affair aftermath and marriage counseling, he wanted to be healthier.

To ride bikes with Jacky and keep up. To live long enough to see his son grow up and become a father himself.

But tonight, he'd seen something horrible. The horror of what a person was capable of doing to another. In his mind, he saw the Millers—dead on the floor of their home. They'd never gotten justice. He hadn't found the killers then. He wondered how likely it would be he'd find the killers who broke into Derrick Winslow's house.

Now he needed something to sink into—to escape. No beer in the fridge. He'd be able to find the chips if he tried. He looked in the bottom cupboards, scanning pots and pans. He took the lid off the rice maker but didn't see anything in it.

Then on top of the fridge, he saw a big strainer Reyna used for noodles. She was more than a foot shorter than he was, so she'd have to pull up a chair or get him to reach it. Maybe she didn't think he'd look there.

He easily pulled it down and saw a brand new, unopened bag of tortilla chips. Somehow, with his lack of confidence in closing a murder case, the find made him feel better about himself.

He stared at the bag for a bit, then put the strainer back in its place.

Adult decision-making sucked. Big time.

He rinsed out his glass and put it on the dish rack.

On the first day of marriage counseling, he'd sat in a room and listened to his wife talk about how disappointed she was with their marriage.

He'd gone in thinking he could write all of it off as her problem. He wanted to—and the easy way to do that was to say *she'd* had the affair. *She'd* betrayed him with Mario Flores, a fellow officer—someone he'd become friends with. *She'd* told her friends she was going to divorce him.

Then in one of their sessions, she'd brought up something she'd never told him: that she'd been sexually assaulted by a man who lived in the house she'd shared with Mateo, not long before he'd "rescued" her after Mateo's arrest. She'd never told Ruiz about the assault, keeping it to herself for all of their marriage. It both broke his heart and frustrated him. It had affected her deeply and their marriage, too. But he couldn't do a damn thing to fix it.

But there was truth in things Reyna had said about him. He had to be honest with himself. He did have things to work on—even if changing only benefitted himself or whoever else he ended up with. Or Jacky.

Reyna had said she wanted to try counseling. He wasn't sure how honest her commitment had been; maybe she just couldn't afford to move out on her own.

But he'd chosen to stay.

If there was a chance things could get better, he wanted to stick around to see it happen.

When Ruiz got to the station the next morning, Grasso was already on the phone, thanks to her short commute.

From the sound of her conversation, she was talking to

other departments, following up on home invasion cases she'd seen in the database.

She looked up at him and waved, as she took a sip of coffee.

"This was three years ago, right? Can you describe what the house was like when you arrived, detective?"

She was jotting down notes on a tablet.

"And you mentioned a shooting. Any fatalities?"

Ruiz poured himself some coffee, dumped in cream and allowed himself one packet of sugar today. He needed to perk up fast.

Today he'd look into Derrick Winslow. He googled the man's name and waited to see the results.

The first thing that came up was a photo of the man smiling confidently on the cover of *Entrepreneurship* magazine. Tanned face, a dark mustache, and a receding hairline. He wore a white suit and sat on a café chair on the deck of a ship.

The article talked about how Winslow was in the business of founding tech companies. He was something called a venture builder. His company provided the funds for a company to launch—like a venture capital firm—but also brought their expertise to new startups. Sometimes even coming up with the initial concept for the company. Then the venture builder helped the startup through each stage of their growth. When the startup company was sold or went public, the venture builder got a big return on the investment.

Winslow had done this dozens of times so far, with his venture builder firm, GrowGo. He was worth more than 50 million dollars. In the article, he made a pitch for entrepreneurs interested in his company.

All of this bored the hell out of Ruiz, and he was by

nature a cynic. So, he continued poking around for any hint of scandal or wrongdoing in the man's life.

He wasn't disappointed.

More personal stats on Derrick Winslow showed that he'd been married and divorced. He had one child, Justin, who was now in college.

But apparently, the guy had a problem keeping it in his pants. During the "Me Too" movement, his name was mentioned by a number of up-and-coming women in tech, as someone who'd harassed or treated them inappropriately.

Two years ago, Derrick Winslow was sued for sexual harassment at one of the startup companies he'd help build. The woman, Natalie Chen, had served as Vice President of Sales and Marketing at a telemarketing software startup, CallerNine—a company Winslow had helped launch. She claimed he'd propositioned her repeatedly and when she refused him and told others about his actions, he retaliated by firing her from the startup. The jury awarded her $1.5 million.

Judging by the results of his Google session, Derrick Winslow was an ass. But he didn't deserve the horrific death he received. It was his and Grasso's job to find the person or persons responsible.

At 9:30, Grasso met him in the conference room to touch base.

"I've got a couple of recent cases in California we might want to take a look at." She took a seat at the table and set her tablet down.

Ruiz wondered how helpful these would be, seeing as his search after the Miller invasion came up with nothing. "I've been looking into Derrick Winslow. He was worth over 50 million. He has a reputation for sexual harassment. One of his startup company managers sued him and won 1.5 million in damages last year."

Grasso looked across the table at him. "Okay, there could be women who'd want him dead. But this was a home invasion."

Ruiz nodded and scrolled through his notes. "There are a lot of similarities between the Miller and Winslow murders. And they took place less than a half a mile away from each other. We have to take that seriously."

"That's what I was looking for—similar crimes in Northern California." Grasso looked down at her notes. "Here's what I found this morning. These were the closest matches. There was a home invasion two years ago down in Salinas. Mostly electronics stolen, and it seems like the assailants just walked right in. No break in. Two roommates were killed, shot as they surprised the assailants. Then in Mill Valley up in Marin County six months ago, two masked gunmen forcibly entered a house, stole electronics and some expensive art, and ransacked the owner's study looking for something. When the owner confronted them, they shot him. He played dead and survived."

Ruiz thought about this. "It's worth it to check out the Marin case. See if we can talk to the survivor." The Marin robbery would have more in common with what they'd seen in Monte Verde. "I still want to talk to Winslow's former manager, Natalie Chen, and Justin, his son."

"When do we hear from crime scene?" Grasso asked.

"Late today or tomorrow morning. I hope Winslow's killer did us a favor and left something behind for us." Based on his experience, Ruiz wasn't optimistic. "The Millers' didn't."

THAT MORNING, Ruiz and Grasso walked to their first interview. Today they'd speak with the man Winslow had co-founded GrowGo Studio with, in downtown Monte Verde.

From the station, they walked three blocks to the small, red brick building on the corner of Main and Milford streets. When Ruiz had heard about Winslow's company, which built and launched startup tech companies, he'd expected the building to be a lot bigger.

The front window of the building, which Ruiz remembered used to be a French laundry, spelled out GrowGo. Below there was an abstract symbol which looked like a tree, with curving roots and branches.

An assistant led Ruiz and Grasso back to the office of co-founder Michael Fisk. Ruiz blinked as soon as he entered the room, as if it were lit by the blinding lights used for nighttime road work. Everything in the office was white. White walls, white furniture and hanging lights. Even the art on the wall, which was mostly abstract black painted shapes, was framed in white.

Fisk looked to be around 50, ten years older than Ruiz himself. He had a receding hairline, and his clear glasses frames made his face look paler and magnified his watery grey eyes. His co-founder had been brutally murdered the night before, but you wouldn't know that by looking at Fisk. He looked calm, completely absorbed in what was happening on the three large computer monitors on this desk.

"Good morning, Mr. Fisk. I'm Detective James Ruiz, and this is my partner, Detective Dani Grasso."

Michael Fisk looked up at them. "Please take a seat. Let me send off this spreadsheet."

He tapped on his keyboard, then turned away from the monitor.

"Where do most of the employees work at your company, Mr. Fisk?" Ruiz asked. "I assumed your company would have a bigger headquarters."

Fisk smiled. "Most of it takes place virtually. We have the main office here, mostly for in-person meetings of startup staff. Derrick had his home office, where we also held meetings and did strategy retreats. Then we have a network of tech and marketing specialists, many of them in other parts of the country, working from home or their offices. They're all experts in skills needed to set up a company, launch it and sell it. We're a venture builder. Are you familiar with that term, Detective?"

Ruiz looked over at Grasso, whose eyes looked glazed over. She shook her head.

"No, not at all," Grasso responded. "I heard your company has something to do with startups."

Fisk smiled, somewhat condescendingly, in Ruiz's opinion.

"Well, yes. We create companies at GrowGo. We generate concepts for startups, find entrepreneurs willing to take them on and we staff them. We provide funding and then draw on our network of experts to build the company from the ground up. As it grows, we help the company navigate the challenges at each stage. Then when the time comes, we help them exit—that is either to sell to a buyer or to go public."

Ruiz started to get the concept. "Like having a baby then helping it grow up, then launching it off into the world."

Fisk nodded curtly. "A decent analogy, Detective Ruiz."

"Were you and Derrick Winslow both in charge of

making the decisions at GrowGo?" Grasso asked. "How did you work together? Was either one of you the CEO?"

"Not really. We were co-founders. I come from the tech side, so I'm more involved with the technical parts of the startup—development, coding and testing. Derrick's background is—*was*—marketing and sales."

"Tough to lose someone you worked so closely with," Ruiz said, watching Fisk's eyes for any emotion. "Where does that leave you now?"

Fisk sighed heavily and shook his head, but his eyes looked dull and unmoved, which seemed odd to Ruiz. "I'll be relying on our specialist network for help. I'm trying to sort things out for the short term this morning. We have one startup we were preparing for an exit—selling to a Chinese-owned company. Another in the intense beginning stage, where we'd just hired an entrepreneur to lead one of our concepts for a startup."

"With your constant communication with Winslow, did you notice anything different about him in the past day or two?" Grasso asked. "Did he seem worried to you? Nervous?"

"Not at all." Fisk said matter-of-factly. "He was acting like he always did. Derrick was a professional, even though we had some differences between us."

Grasso jumped right on this comment. "What do you mean by differences, Mr. Fisk?"

Fisk looked like he'd regretted what he just said. "Derrick had soft spots for some things. It caused a few problems."

Ruiz and Grasso exchanged glances.

"We heard about the harassment lawsuit," Ruiz nodded. "Natalie Chen. What can you tell us about that?"

"Detective, I can't discuss that." Fisk stiffened. "And I

won't. Let's just say that Derrick made some mistakes. Like human beings do. And he paid for them."

Ruiz thought that was an understatement; from the news reports, Derrick had a track record. He'd aggressively harassed Ms. Chen, and he hadn't been remorseful about it.

Grasso was frowning and looked like she wanted to speak up about something, but finally sighed, closed her mouth, and looked down at her tablet.

Ruiz thought of the free access the killer had apparently had to Winslow's place. "As far as you know, who had access to the house?"

"Winslow's house is large, with a big outdoor deck. And a great room that we used for meetings. When we bring our entrepreneurs and experts into town, we often used his place as an onsite campus," Fisk said. "It was open during the day because there were so many people coming and going. A lot of meetings. It really worried the housekeeper, so he'd been locking the entrances when she left at four."

In Ruiz's experience, the observations of housekeepers and personal assistants tended to provide very helpful information after a crime. Their next appointment would be with Olga Kostenko, Winslow's housekeeper. She could hopefully fill in the blanks as far as what was taken in the robbery.

"Did Winslow keep anything valuable in plain sight in his home? Art, computer equipment, jewelry?" Ruiz asked.

Fisk nodded, then his expression sobered. "Winslow liked to show off his wealth. Not sure where that came from, but he enjoyed people seeing that he'd acquired a lot. Strange what he could be stingy about and what he would spend lavishly on. The two of us were very different people."

"Was there anything in particular that someone might want to steal?" Grasso asked.

Fisk thought for a moment. "He had some expensive pieces of art. A painting by one of the minor French impressionists. That's what comes to mind, off the top of my head."

"Where were you the night of Mr. Winslow's death, Mr. Fisk?" Grasso asked it, a bold look in her eyes.

Fisk paled and looked taken aback. "I was at home. I live in Scotts Valley, about 45 minutes away. My wife Beth and I were streaming a movie from 9 to about 11 p.m. Then I had to make a call to one of our startups in Ireland to troubleshoot something."

Ruiz asked for the contact information for the startup, so Fisk looked it up on his phone and printed the phone number neatly on a post-it from his desk.

He handed it to Ruiz. "I was talking to Conor Doyle—our entrepreneur in place at that startup. He's working with the company till it's sold."

"There were a lot of people coming and going at Winslow's house." Ruiz said. "Can you think of anyone your firm's been working with who might have had a problem with Winslow?"

Fisk's phone rang, and he glanced anxiously at it. "Derrick had strong opinions. But most people respected his experience and were grateful for the opportunity to work with him."

Ruiz thanked Michael Fisk for his time and handed him his card. Fisk's assistant escorted him and Grasso out. Outside the building, Grasso shot a look at Ruiz. She was not happy.

"So, Winslow hitting on one of his executives was just 'being *human*.'"

"Disturbing if that was the way of thinking at GrowGo." Ruiz raised his eyebrows. "Might be worth it to talk to Natalie Chen. If only to find out more about Winslow."

**6**

———

I t took Ruiz a couple of hours to track the woman down.

Since her firing three years ago from GrowGo's telemarketing startup, CallerNine, Natalie Chen had worked at multiple companies in Silicon Valley. Ruiz went through her list of employers on LinkedIn, which hadn't been updated. One of the woman's friends at the last listed company told him Natalie had started a marketing consulting firm in Mountain View, near the Google campus.

Ruiz and Grasso picked up burritos at Garcia's for a late lunch at 1:30. Then Ruiz followed San Antonio Road to Middlefield, then turned onto Charleston.

They pulled into the small strip of parking slots in front of the office building, which looked like it had been remodeled from a 1960s medical office building. Natalie Chen's firm shared the building with a financial advisor's office and an academic tutoring service. Ruiz was glad he'd written down the name of her company. *Utter Brilliance Marketing.* Natalie Chen's name didn't appear anywhere.

Grasso laughed when she read the name on the sign. "Pretty ballsy to call her company that. I love it."

Grasso had finished half her carne asada burrito and wrapped the rest in the foil wrapper. Ruiz decided he couldn't finish his either and wrapped it up. He used to polish off one of Garcia's burritos in ten minutes and still be hungry.

They entered the office to find a small waiting area, with inviting-looking chairs and business and marketing magazines fanned out on end tables. Before they could sit down, a woman dressed in a bright floral jumpsuit came out from a room in the back to greet them. She was gorgeous.

"Detective James Ruiz, from Monte Verde PD." Ruiz started in. "And my partner, Detective Dani Grasso. We're here to ask you some questions about Derrick Winslow."

Natalie Chen sucked in her breath. "Okay, then." She clasped her hands together as if she were taking a moment to think, then she smiled. "Let's go back to my office. Can I get you anything to drink? Bottled water? Fresh squeezed juice?"

"No thanks, Ms. Chen." Ruiz nodded. "We just came from lunch. Where can we talk?"

She led them through a door into her office, which was decorated with bright splashes of color and lined with white boards listing projects. There were more comfortable chairs here. Ruiz sunk down into one of the chairs and felt like his body was supported and almost massaged. He noticed Grasso closed her eyes and sighed as soon as she sat down.

Grasso leaned forward. "Ms. Chen, these chairs are amazing."

Natalie Chen flashed a smile and looked around the room.

"I think it's important to provide a comfortable space for

my staff. The more at ease they are, the better the ideas flow. Thanks to the damages I was awarded, I could afford to make this the place I wanted it to be."

Ruiz could see the woman was nervous but trying to hide it. She had the look of someone who was considering very carefully what to say.

"I heard the news this morning about Derrick." She sat down in the executive chair in front of her desk. "I can't say I'm sad that he's dead."

"Ms. Chen, can you tell me where you were last night, between 7 p.m. and 11 p.m.?"

Natalie Chen gasped. She did it so quietly he barely heard it. Then she smiled. "Of course. I was at home. Eating takeout and binge-watching *Game of Thrones*. That's how exciting my life is."

"Do you have anyone who can verify that?" Ruiz asked firmly.

"My neighbor upstairs would have heard I was home. Alec Higa. He's in unit 10. I'm at Park Square in Cupertino. It's a nice condo complex, but you can hear everybody."

"I know that complex," Grasso said suddenly. Ruiz wondered if that was near her condo, though she obviously wasn't spending time there now. "So, you didn't leave at any time last night?"

"I didn't. I had a pizza delivered late, which you can verify." She closed her eyes to think. "From Rocco's. It was delivered around 9 p.m."

Ruiz continued. Everything about Natalie Chen's answers was a little too perfect.

"You were awarded 1.5 million in your harassment suit against Winslow. This was how long ago?"

"A year ago. He and Fisk gaslighted me, trying to act like what Winslow did was normal. I wanted to be vindicated.

Because of how much money meant to Derrick, that was the way to do it."

"If I could ask—what did he do to you, Ms. Chen?" Grasso's voice was sympathetic.

"He made my life hell for a year. He had my phone number, since we worked closely together during training. He texted me selfies of his favorite body part. He scheduled meetings, and then it turned out—big surprise—it was only him and me in the meeting. He followed me into the restroom when I was working late and pinned me against a stall door and groped me. After I brought it up to HR, Derrick told them I'd made it all up as revenge for a bad review he gave me. I was fired. Fortunately, I documented everything."

Natalie Chen's calm exterior had cracked, and she looked and sounded angry. Ruiz knew from things his wife Reyna had said in marriage counseling that she'd dealt with similar situations with men. Before that he'd had no idea how often this happened to women. Natalie Chen had received her money, but he could see the scars from her interactions with Winslow remained. He wondered if she were angry enough to kill him.

"I am sorry you had to go through that," Ruiz said quietly. "How do you feel about Mr. Winslow now, Ms. Chen? Were you still angry at him?"

She shook her head. "I haven't been for a while. I did what I needed to do—win the suit. Then I moved on."

"I can't say I didn't learn useful things from Winslow." Chen leaned back in her chair, picked up her glass of green, healthy-looking juice and took a sip. "He was a smart guy— a basic, old-school marketer, all about changing people's perceptions. He'd make sure we got subtle messages out there in the marketplace with lots of stories—real people

talking about their experiences. Winslow created a truth—
let's say it's that only *this* chair will help your back
problems." She tapped the arms of her chair.

"Then he put it out there in the media to make sure
everyone was surrounded by it. So, when we launched,
everyone already believed it—our product *was* different. He
was doing that with CallerNine. By the time we released, he
made sure that the message was out there: existing
telemarketing systems were timewasters, full of problems,
and ours was designed differently. He seeded those ideas all
over publications, conferences, and social media. People
began to believe the message. I was in awe of how well he
did it."

"Isn't that just—lying?" Grasso asked. "On a really big
scale?"

Natalie laughed. "Not necessarily. Marketing is a tool to
use to get your message out. It can be used for good or bad
purposes. Maybe what you have to sell people is a really
great product. Something that could genuinely help them."

"Let's go back to the chair example." She smiled,
pointing to the ones they were sitting in. "You guys are
pretty comfortable, right? Let's say you designed an
innovative new type of chair, because you feel sorry for
people with back problems. You put a message out there
saying that this chair, which you have to sit in eight hours a
day, is designed to keep you from having back problems. A
traditional chair won't give you the proper support, so you're
going to have back problems. Bad chair. Don't buy it. So, if
people hear that from several different sources, they will
start to believe it's true."

"Sure. I can see how that works now." Grasso nodded.

"Ms. Chen, when was the last time you saw Mr.
Winslow?" Ruiz asked.

Natalie Chen swallowed and looked down at her hands which Ruiz noticed were trembling slightly. "Last week. I gave a sales pitch at a startup expo in Sunnyvale. I saw him in the hall on my way to my talk. I didn't know he was going to be there, but for what his company does, it made sense."

"Did he see you? Did he say anything to you?" Ruiz asked gently.

She shook her head. Her composure seemed to return, and her voice was calmer. "I saw him and walked in the opposite direction. I didn't see him in the presentation, thank God."

"Ms. Chen, you've been through a difficult experience, but I'd like to ask you a little bit more about your experience with GrowGo and its founders," Grasso asked. "How did you end up working with them?"

"Derrick hired me for CallerNine as the head of sales and marketing," she said. "In a way, what GrowGo does is similar to producing a play. They come up with an idea for a startup company—the script for the play. In our case, it was fully integrated telemarketing software. Then they hire people for all the management positions, the actors who play their parts. That was me, Jeff Gabbard, our CEO, and Rich Tankian, our manager of software development. Then with the advice of Michael and Derrick and a few other industry experts, we built our company. After about a year and a half, it went live. Show time. Then GrowGo worked with CallerNine as they scaled up. As they became a larger company."

"Did you report to Derrick Winslow?" Grasso asked.

"I reported to Jeff, but I was being trained by Derrick. I sat in on a lot of meetings with Michael, too, as a manager for the startup."

"How did Michael and Derrick get along?" Ruiz asked.

"Badly." She let out a sharp laugh. "They disagreed on a lot. When I was there, it was becoming a joke. They fought a lot. Maybe it's just my perspective, but Derrick seemed to undermine Michael's authority whenever he could."

"And how did Michael Fisk react to that?" Ruiz asked.

"In my opinion? He let Derrick walk all over him for too long. He didn't want to confront him. He's a tech guy. He's happiest when he's working with coders and developers." Chen raised her eyebrows and shook her head.

Ruiz and Grasso thanked Natalie Chen for her cooperation and left her with their cards.

Ruiz turned on the car, and Grasso dug in the bag for the last half of her burrito.

"I wouldn't think she's a suspect, but we need to check her alibi with the upstairs neighbor." Ruiz said, as he backed out and headed for San Antonio Road. "Interesting what she said about Fisk and Winslow. We need to talk to Gabbard, her boss. And a few other people who've worked with GrowGo."

Grasso nodded her head, her mouth full. After a few seconds she spoke.

"I don't see her staging a home invasion. I think she was being very honest about her feelings for Winslow. She wasn't sad he was dead."

After she went back to wrap up some paperwork at the station at 6 p.m., Grasso drove back to her old neighborhood in Cupertino and knocked on Alec Higa's door. He'd said he heard dishes being put in the dishwasher and loud, dramatic music from the TV in the apartment directly below from 9 till 11 p.m. It was annoying but he was used to it. Chen watched a lot of TV.

On her way back to Tom's house, Grasso thought about their interview with Natalie Chen.

She'd never been stalked or harassed, like Natalie Chen. She'd never thought of herself as someone that could happen to. She was attractive, she thought, but not in a way that would make a man fall over himself to send her a "selfie of his favorite body part." She was grateful for that.

She clicked to open the garage and pulled the Mini Cooper inside. Right before she turned off the car, her phone rang, transferring over to the Bluetooth. She recognized her grandfather's number.

"*Buona sera*, Unnon." She decided to take the call in the car.

"Daniela, it's so good to hear your voice. I got your message about coming for dinner with your friend—"

"My boyfriend, Tom," she added quickly.

"Yes, I am very excited to meet this young man of yours —Tom."

She didn't correct him there; she didn't quite know what to say. At least he was younger than Unnon.

"I want you to meet him. He's a good man."

"Let's say this Thursday. You come at 6. We'll eat and drink."

She heard the struggle in his voice to form and remember the words, probably the result of his stroke last year.

Yet another complicated family feeling—pity, along with her frustration with him and her fucked-up family dynamics. Along with love. Life would be much easier if you could feel only one emotion at a time.

"That works. *Grazie,* Unnon. Tom and I will see you then."

## 7

Dani grabbed her mug and tablet and headed for the conference room, passing by Frank Ladera's desk on the way.

This morning he'd brought in a pink box of donuts from Sam's in Santa Clara, the best glazed donuts you could find in the valley. You had to call ahead to reserve your box. She wasn't usually a fan of a sweet breakfast, but these were exquisite. And Frank was nowhere to be seen.

She picked one up with a napkin and continued on her way. Every once in a while, Frank would put a lavish treat out, in an attempt to lure people over to talk to him. A win for her that he wasn't at his desk—he was probably in with the captain or in the restroom. She'd scored a donut without having to make conversation with him.

She sat down to comb databases for new home invasion matches.

Ruiz came in late, since he'd helped Jacky transport his fourth-grade California history diorama to class and set it up.

When she suddenly realized Ruiz was right behind her, she jumped.

"Guilty conscience? You shouldn't steal things from Ladera's desk." He gave her a stern look as he spotted her donut. Then he grinned. "You up for a road trip to Marin County?"

They took a Prius from the back lot. Ruiz put his Starbucks cup in the cupholder, and they headed for 280 North, glad for the opportunity to get out. The sky had cleared after being overcast for two days.

Grasso pressed her nose up against the window like a kid. There was no place like the peninsula when the hills were green from the winter rains. The radar dishes on the hills above Stanford University tilted upwards to the blue sky as if sunning themselves. Yellow mustard flowers dotted the green areas, making it look like spring, even though it still felt cold enough to be winter.

There were two routes north to the Golden Gate Bridge to Marin—highway 101 and highway 280. Drab 101 was a workhorse of a freeway. It followed the edge of the San Francisco Bay, going through industrial, non-photogenic parts of peninsula cities, past sprawling San Francisco International Airport and cutting through downtown San Francisco.

Highway 280 wound through the scenic rolling hills of the peninsula, then led you along the western part of San Francisco to the Golden Gate Bridge. It was a longer drive than 101, but Grasso took 280 whenever she could.

"Schallert told me about when the Queen of England came to the Bay Area years ago," Ruiz said, as he sped up and passed a slow-moving pickup truck. "They took her in a motorcade from Stanford to San Francisco on 280. There was no way they'd let her see 101. He calls 280 the Queen's highway."

Within an hour, they could see the Golden Gate Bridge and beyond it the green headlands of Marin. Today they'd interview the detective and the victim about the home invasion that had the most similarities to the Millers' and Derrick Winslow's.

"What did you find when you looked into the Miller case?" Grasso said as she turned away from the window. "You haven't talked much about it."

"I talked to jurisdictions all over the state. There was a robbery up in Hillsborough and we thought that might be tied to the Millers' invasion. But they made an arrest after two weeks. Grilled the guys, and they swore they had nothing to do with it. Said they weren't killers. Turns out they weren't in the area the night when the Millers were killed."

"You kept looking for a while."

"What I saw that night—it stuck with me. I still see the bodies. It was hard to let go of that case. I still had hope that somehow, I could find the guys who did it."

"And you say that I'm too much of an optimist." Grasso turned to him and grinned.

They drove over the Golden Gate, feeling the strong wind push against the car, as they enjoyed the bright blue sky surrounding them on the bridge. Once they passed by the green headlands of Marin, they took the East Blithedale exit for Mill Valley.

The narrow road led them to the heart of the town, past quaint California bungalows and small, wood-shingled homes that looked like they'd been built in the 1920s or 30s. Mt. Tamalpais, a low-sloped mountain, hung grey-green in the background like a theatre backdrop.

At the station, after signing in, a detective took them back to a meeting room.

"Grasso, Ruiz, I'm Detective Mark Daley. I worked the home invasion case over on Edgewood last year. I understand your situation, and I'm happy to tell you about the case and the methods used."

"The case is still open?"

"Unfortunately." Daley looked at them grimly. "We traced a couple of the stolen items. Looks like they were transported out of the state. Like Monte Verde, this is a wealthy area, and our residents are often targeted. We don't think the people who did this were locals."

Grasso put her hands on the table. "Can you tell us about the crime scene when you showed up? What did you notice?"

"No signs of forced entry. It seemed like these guys just walked in. We think they'd been watching the house and knew that the door would be unlocked in the early evenings. Electronics were taken, but in this particular house, there was an art collection and the individuals involved seemed to know its worth. Paintings and sculptures were taken. We found one of them for sale at an art auction in upstate New York a few months later. The homeowner's office was a mess; papers were rifled through."

"And there was a shooting," Grasso asked. "The homeowner was shot?"

"The homeowner came in from the backyard and heard noises in the house. He was shot in the stomach and fell and then played dead till the robbers left. He survived and was able to give us some info on what he saw. He said he saw two men dressed in black t-shirts. He also thought he saw a delivery van in his driveway."

"We'd like to talk to him." Grasso said, and Daley sat down to look up contact info.

Grasso looked over at Ruiz. He didn't look very excited.

"What are you thinking?"

"Let's talk to him." Ruiz sat back in his seat and rested his chin on his hand. "But the invasions in Monte Verde seem different. The murders seemed part of the job—it was as important to kill the residents of the house as it was to steal the goods. All of them took place in bedrooms. In the case here, the guy was shot, but it was because he'd run out after the perps."

Daley nodded. "You're thinking the residents themselves were targeted."

"I've been thinking about the Miller case over and over for five years." Ruiz sighed and took a sip of his Starbucks vanilla latte, which Grasso thought must be lukewarm by now.

"It's hard to let go. These things stay with you like ghosts. They'll mess with you until you move on," Daley said. "Best of luck to you, man. Let me know if there are any more questions I can answer for you."

Out in the sun again, Grasso and Ruiz walked to the Prius.

"I'm sorry that wasn't more helpful." Grasso waited for the beep to unlock, then pulled open the passenger car door.

"Actually, it was." Ruiz did a leg stretch in front of the car door before he opened it. She knew his long legs tended to cramp up on long car rides. "Let's talk to the survivor and see what he says. We might want to approach this case differently."

Within ten minutes, they were at the house of 85-year-old Oscar Williams on Edgewood Drive.

The small elderly man described the night of the home invasion, and by the look in his eyes, it had made him more angry than scared.

"The worst part was the guys came into my house like they owned the place." Oscar spoke with some accent from the East Coast, which area exactly Grasso wasn't sure.

"Two guys. Young guys. All wearing black t-shirts and jeans. They just walked in and started taking stuff—my art, my sculptures, my TV. I came in from the backyard when I heard them and told them to get the hell out of my house. Then one of them shot me—" He grabbed his stomach and folded over, while making a dramatic *uhhh* sound. "Like that. Well, the only thing I could do is fall over and play dead until they went away."

"Did you see their car or vehicle?" Grasso asked, amused at the old man's acting out his attack. This guy had the charm of her grandfather. Like her grandfather, Oscar Williams seemed tough.

The old man shook his head. "I tried to run to the window, but by that time, I'd lost a lot of blood and my head was spinning. I saw something parked in the driveway that looked like a van. Then I passed out."

After a hurried fast-food lunch, they headed for Scotts Valley in the Santa Cruz Mountains.

This time Grasso took the wheel of the Prius, which Ruiz noticed had used a ridiculously small amount of gas on their drive to Marin.

It became clear that they'd chosen the worst time of day possible.

They hit the last of the commuter traffic going back over the hill on Highway 17. With the sluggishness of the traffic, Ruiz was happy to sit back and let Grasso drive.

They were due to interview Beth Fisk at the Fisks' home. Michael was still at the office and Beth had told them he had a meeting and wouldn't be back till 8 p.m.

They wanted to check Michael's alibi. He'd told them he'd been exercising in his personal gym behind his house, then he'd talked to the director of software development at one of their startups in Ireland—Conor Doyle.

Scotts Valley was a community set in the redwoods, a halfway point between San Jose and coastal Santa Cruz. If there hadn't been so much traffic, Ruiz thought, it would have been a pretty drive through the mountains. Redwoods and fir trees on both sides of the road. On their left, they saw Lexington Reservoir. Its level looked low, even though they were supposedly in the rainy season.

They turned off on Scotts Valley Boulevard, past a shopping center and into a suburban area of the city.

Derrick Winslow had lived in a large, sprawling house in one of the most expensive areas of Monte Verde.

Michael and Beth Fisk lived in a cheery, yellow ranch-style, on a small street, surrounded by closely set houses that looked a lot like it. Fisk's commute into Monte Verde must take him forty-five minutes, Ruiz estimated. Winslow, on the other hand, usually didn't have to leave his house. If he did, it was a quick drive to GrowGo's offices in downtown Monte Verde.

Interesting that Fisk and Winslow were supposedly equal partners in GrowGo, yet they seemed to live very different lifestyles. He wondered if Winslow held a larger share in the business.

Ruiz would lead in the questioning. He'd always been good in interviews with older women and seemed to quickly earn their trust. Grasso was happy to let him do it.

Ruiz rapped on the door, and a petite woman in her forties, with glasses and short, bleached blond hair, came to the door.

"Good afternoon, detectives." Beth Fisk greeted them with a friendly smile and invited them into her living room, which was furnished with brown furniture and a lot of golden brown oak wood. "Please have a seat. Can I get you anything to drink?"

Both Ruiz and Grasso shook their heads. "Thank you, Mrs. Fisk," Ruiz nodded. "We're here to get some background information on your husband and also ask you about your husband's experience at GrowGo with Derrick Winslow."

Beth Fisk frowned as she took a seat across from them. She had a look of someone who taught school, maybe elementary school. She looked like some of the teachers Jacky'd had.

"I'd like to ask you, detectives—" she pressed her fingers together. "Are you saying the attack on Derrick's house was a robbery? A home invasion? They've been calling it that on the news."

It was a fair question. "Items were taken from the house that night while Derrick Winslow was there," Ruiz said. "But the murder is our focus right now."

"You and Michael were home that night?" Ruiz asked the woman, who began nodding.

"Michael worked in Monte Verde till about 5, then came back over the hill and we had dinner together. Kaiden, our son, who's a student at UC Santa Cruz, decided to come for dinner. Probably because he'd spent his food budget for the month," she said, her mouth twisting wryly.

"Your husband told us he was working out in his home gym that evening," Grasso said.

"That's true. He worked out after dinner, so by the time we finished chatting with Kaiden, it would have been about 8:30 when he got started."

"Mr. Fisk said his workouts are all tracked, so he'd have the time recorded." Grasso said.

Beth Fisk smiled proudly. "Absolutely. Michael's a device geek. He's not happy unless all the data's connected. So, his workouts are recorded by his fitness system and synced up with his phone and wellness apps. I'm sure he could show you."

"So that night, he worked out for how long, would you say?" Ruiz asked. He noticed the smile beginning to fade from the woman's face.

Beth Fisk paused for a moment. From her expression, Ruiz had just insulted her family name.

"It sounds like you're accusing my husband of murder, detective." Behind her glasses, her round brown eyes burned with fury. "There's nobody less likely to commit violence than Michael. He's a sweetheart. He's incapable of hurting anyone."

Grasso jumped in. "Mrs. Fisk, we have to ask these questions of anyone who had a close relationship with Derrick Winslow. Your husband was his business partner."

Ruiz nodded in agreement. "Standard procedure, Mrs. Fisk. So how long did he work out?"

Beth Fisk backed off but still looked uneasy. "He normally works out on his equipment for an hour—cycling, treadmill, and weights. He's a creature of habit, and the world would have to end for him to change his routine. I'm sure it was an hour."

"Any other activities that night?"

Beth Fisk paused as she thought about this. "He handles calls in different time zones late at night. He's often up late making calls to Europe and Asia."

"He told us about a call to a startup in Ireland that night."

Beth looked visibly relieved. She brushed her bangs off her face. "Well, that must have been it, then. I went to bed at 10 since I teach second grade and get up before the sun. Michael lives the tech life and sleeps in till nine. He came to bed around midnight-12:30."

That would have given Fisk a decent window of time to get to Monte Verde and back.

"Mrs. Fisk, how did your husband get along with Derrick Winslow?" Grasso asked. "Would you say they were on good terms?"

"They'd known each other since college," Beth Fisk said. "Michael and Derrick were very different. Derrick was the extrovert, always schmoozing. Always talking a big story and coming up with the master plan. Michael was—well, the geek. He had the technical expertise. The software development background. He was precise, detailed and a lot more responsible than Derrick. They complemented each other and stayed together with GrowGo, but it's been a rough four years."

"Any fallings out recently—arguments or disagreements?"

"Of course," she snapped, as if it should be obvious to them. "They had to work together in order to keep the startups going. They argued and fought all the time.

Michael ended up giving in, just because Derrick could be so bullheaded. Derrick didn't give in easily."

Grasso caught Ruiz's eye. Beth Fisk seemed very protective of her husband.

"If you have any questions or can think of anything that might be helpful in the investigation, please let us know." Grasso handed Beth Fisk one of her cards.

They headed out into the dark, for what would hopefully be a shorter drive back to Monte Verde.

As Grasso drove, Ruiz stretched his legs out and thought about the woman's answers.

"Beth Fisk seemed on edge."

"Maybe she wasn't sure about her husband's whereabouts that night." Grasso said, as she clicked on the brights for the dark stretch of road they passed through before they reached the highway. "My guess is, she didn't know if her husband was there or not after she went to bed."

Ruiz nodded. "I wanted to look at you when she told us the time she went to bed and the time he came to bed. That was enough time to get to Monte Verde, kill his co-founder and steal his stuff, and head back to Scotts Valley."

"We need to verify that phone call to Ireland." Ruiz leaned his seat back, so he could stretch his legs out further. "We need something to substantiate that Fisk's telling the truth.

AFTER THE TWO DETECTIVES LEFT, Beth Fisk sat down on the couch and put up her legs.

Her varicose veins had been driving her crazy. Teaching wasn't a profession for the weak. Six hours of standing in front of a class of thirty-two second graders five days a week wasn't doing her legs any favors.

She plumped up the couch pillows to rest her legs on, then lay down and let out a huge sigh of relief.

Derrick Winslow was dead. *Hallelujah.*

Somebody had blown the lecherous, narcissistic ass's face off.

Ever since she'd read the article online in the *San Jose Mercury-News*, the thought of it cheered her up. If she knew how to dance, she'd do it right here in the living room, despite her throbbing legs. No other news could make her this happy.

For five years, she'd played nursemaid to Michael's wounded ego, every time he came home from a day of being bullied by Derrick Winslow. The two had been college buddies years ago and had reconnected at a conference—both interested in finding a new way to launch tech startups.

But it soon became clear to Beth that Michael's relationship with his new business partner was unhealthy. Winslow needed to appear the top dog in every situation, at the expense of others. Especially Michael.

Every compliment turned into a twist, a dig that managed to home in on some weakness of Michael's. Derrick made Michael the butt of jokes in meetings, which trickled down into disrespectful treatment from the people working in GrowGo's startups.

She'd seen the effect on her husband; instead of standing up to Derrick and telling him the digs were unacceptable, Michael chose to plunge more deeply into his work, pretending it didn't bother him. When she'd asked him about this, he told her he was taking the "high road."

Not what *she* would do. She would have told Derrick

Winslow to shut the fuck up, whether anyone else was in the room or not.

But then couples are often paired up with complementary gifts. She spoke her mind; Michael avoided confrontation. Michael set up the wi-fi, computers and paid all the bills; she resolved complaints, returned things to stores and got rid of pesky door-to-door salesmen—all things Michael hated to do.

She'd gone into marriage knowing it would be a team effort. Her expectations had been realistic, and she hadn't been disappointed.

When she'd read reports of a home invasion, she'd been relieved—jubilant—that karma had come to Derrick Winslow, in the form of random assailants who happened to be looking for a pricey house to rob.

But the detectives' questions tonight worried her. They seemed to be focusing on people with actual motives for murdering Winslow. They wanted detailed info on Michael's movements the night of the murder, details that she wasn't 100 percent sure of.

She stood up from the couch and moved to the window, curious to see if the detectives had left. She parted the curtains slightly to check. She was relieved to see that their car was gone.

And while Michael seemed the least likely person she knew to commit a murder, she knew the truth: Michael could not have lasted a week longer as Derrick's partner at GrowGo.

**8**

———

Detective Mario Flores, San Jose Homicide, stood in front of the mirror in his bathroom, examining the mustache he'd been growing for the past month.

Today he was shaving it off.

It lay there on his lip, looking like a dark, fuzzy caterpillar, as his sister Dawn had described it. He hated it. He'd grown it because Kira had told him she loved men with mustaches. They got her *excited,* she said. With that incentive, he grew it out, in a scruffy transitional phase. He'd already received the comments at work.

*Hey, Mario, forget to shave?*

*Been hitting the chocolate milk a little hard there, son?*

Why had it been so important to him? He'd become like some old-timey stereotype of a woman who changes her hairdo to keep her man.

Now that Kira was out of his life, it didn't matter anyway. He'd suspected she was seeing someone else for a while. It drove him crazy. He wanted to grill her, make her tell him who it was. She teased him with talk about being polyamorous. He couldn't stand not knowing where she was or who she was with. Yet he couldn't manage to break it off with her either.

*How far you have fallen, Ro.*

His sister Dawn's snarky voice played in his head. He wanted to remind his sarcastic sister that he made good decisions, too.

He lathered his upper lip and held the razor, carefully gliding it over his lip, and felt it tugging at the hairs. It wasn't a comfortable feeling, but he continued until it looked like he'd gotten everything. He washed his face with cold water, then blotted it with the hand towel.

Fresh, new skin. Soft as a baby's behind.

It was a day for a new start.

He'd closed the Lopez grocery case last week. Tracked down and arrested the killer who'd shot Manny Lopez in his store in downtown San Jose two months ago. Buckley should be pleased with his performance. He'd been working his ass off, trying to pull himself back up to where he'd been. Where he was before he lost his team to Jesperson.

He deserved it. He'd fucked up big time. He'd put his own desire before his job and almost blown the Schuler case. He'd lost the respect of his coworkers, especially Mandy Dirkson, who'd worshipped him for a while. She looked at him in disgust now when she passed through the department to Jesperson's office, which was right next to the one belonging to Buckley, the sergeant he'd reported to directly before the *incident*.

He'd lost his position. He'd lost a friend. For a while, he'd lost his mind.

He realized last year that he'd made a mistake. A series of mistakes. So, he tried to make a change. That should count for something. He'd even lectured Reyna Ruiz after she'd called for his help when her car wouldn't start last year.

He told her to make up her mind about Jimmy—he'd resisted temptation and preached to her from his new position of repentance. He'd gone through hell and back. Only to have his job taken from him and another girlfriend leave him. How long was this going to take?

His sister Dawn—who was a sarcastic Jiminy Cricket conscience to his fun-loving Pinocchio—told him he needed to chill the fuck out.

He dressed for the workday, wearing a blue-grey shirt and a navy tie with yellow flecks that showed off the gold in his brown eyes. He'd ironed his pants himself, making the crease precise and sharp as a knife. He'd whitened his teeth since his constant coffee drinking was taking a toll on his bright smile.

He bared his teeth in the mirror. He could already see an improvement.

He had a meeting with Buckley at 10 a.m. He'd be ready. With a new smile. And eagerness to try again.

And his shiny bright, new baby self.

As soon as he got to the station that morning, Ruiz punched in the number for CallerNine that Natalie Chen had given him.

Since Jeff Gabbard lived nearby in Palo Alto, he volunteered to come by the station for an interview.

He came by at 11:30 a.m., right before lunch. Ruiz walked him back to the interview room.

Jeff Gabbard, CEO of the CallerNine startup, was thin, fit and looked to Ruiz like a salesman and a former athlete—

maybe a tennis player. He had a loose, friendly way of moving. He wore a plaid shirt, fancy jeans, and a casual jacket. Ruiz wondered if Winslow, GrowGo's sales and marketing founder, had been the one to hire him.

"Thanks for coming in, Mr. Gabbard." Grasso greeted him from her seat at the table as the executive came in.

"It was a quick trip, and I'm happy to help in any way I can," he said, taking a seat across from Ruiz. He leaned forward, his hands clasped in front of him. "I've been in shock since I heard the news about Derrick. It's a loss for us and all GrowGo's startups."

"How long has CallerNine been a company, Mr. Gabbard?" Ruiz asked. "When did GrowGo first start your company?"

"GrowGo had the idea for the telemarketing system about four years ago, then put out the concept for the company and listings for positions they were hiring for, to staff the company. I'd wanted the chance to head up a company, and GrowGo offered a unique opportunity to do that, so I applied. Within a month, I was hired as entrepreneur CEO."

"You worked closely with Derrick Winslow." Ruiz was willing to bet Gabbard got along well with Winslow. "Tell me what he was like."

"He was a good mentor." He looked like he was blinking back tears. "We both had sales backgrounds, so we spoke the same language. We hit it off pretty quickly."

"That wasn't the case for Natalie Chen, unfortunately." Ruiz said, and Gabbard's face turned red.

"That was an unfortunate situation." Gabbard pressed his fingers together into a steeple and looked down. "Natalie's a good friend of mine. I know she went through hell that year."

"Did you work with Michael Fisk much?" Grasso asked.

Gabbard nodded. "Of course. He's the best in the industry when it comes to managing software development. I had a lot to learn on the software side. Michael was patient with me and helped me as I worked with the development team."

All Gabbard's answers sounded like neat and tidy testimonials on a sales brochure.

"What was the relationship like between Michael Fisk and Derrick Winslow?" Grasso continued. "From your experience, did they work well together?"

Gabbard's face seemed to drop. He took a few moments before he answered. "They had some disagreements over the course of our work with GrowGo. Sometimes it seemed like there was some big division between them that nobody had told us about. It became confusing. One told us one thing, one another. It was pretty clear they didn't like each other. Which seemed odd to me, since the two of them co-founded the company."

"Why do you think they didn't get along?" Grasso asked. "Was it a particular issue or subject that was a problem?"

Gabbard thought about this. "Maybe they were friends at one time. But from what I saw, Derrick seemed determined to make Michael look bad. Michael ignored him and did what he wanted. The poor communication affected our startup. If I would have known this was the way the studio was run, I would not have signed on with GrowGo. I was pressing Derrick just last week, hoping Caller Nine could exit soon."

Ruiz leaned forward, his eyes intent on Gabbard's face, waiting for the man's more honest assessment of his business mentor.

"How did Winslow take that?" he asked.

Gabbard's face reddened again, and he looked flustered.

"I told him I thought GrowGo couldn't help us anymore. We were ready to go it alone—or to be acquired. He did not take it well." The CEO grimaced. "He told me there was no way we were ready—and that he thought *I* was part of the problem."

"How did you feel after that talk, Mr. Gabbard?"

Gabbard shook his head. His calm, easygoing demeanor was gone now.

"Derrick was gaslighting me. At GrowGo, I had no recourse, nobody else I could talk to about it. I was preparing to make my case in another meeting with him after my business trip next week."

AFTER GABBARD LEFT THE STATION, Grasso and Ruiz sat across from each other in the interrogation room.

"Took him a while to get around to it. At first, you'd think he and Winslow were best buddies." Ruiz looked down at his notes. "But Gabbard had his own grudge against Winslow."

"He's good friends with Natalie Chen, too," Grasso said, as she picked up her phone and checked a text. When she frowned, Ruiz wondered if it was from one of her brothers. "That could be added incentive to get rid of Winslow."

"It looks like Gabbard lives alone," Ruiz said, mentally adding the man to their ongoing list. "Let's figure out where he was the night of the murder."

AT 12:30 P.M., Ruiz received what he'd been waiting for—a

call from Conor Doyle, CEO of the startup PlanCentra in Ireland.

He texted Grasso and asked her to meet him in the interrogation room.

"Conor verified that he'd been doing a troubleshooting session over the phone with Michael Fisk at 6:35 in the morning Dublin time. That would be 10:35 p.m. the night Winslow was killed."

Grasso sat across from him, angling her head as she read through the crime scene report. "Fisk was telling the truth. That's progress. I guess we move on down the list."

She opened her lunch bag and took out a sandwich Tom packed for her this morning—chicken salad, made the good-old fashioned Iowa way, with something called Miracle Whip. It had a weird, sweet taste, but the wheat bread, made by Tom's tenants, the Angwins, was delicious.

Ruiz crunched carrot and celery sticks and finished off his usual sad container of nonfat yogurt while they went over the report.

Fingerprints belonged to Winslow mainly and his housekeeper, Olga Kostenko. Winslow lived alone, as far as they knew, so it made sense. Multiple sets of fingerprints were found in the conference room downstairs. Not a surprise, with all the GrowGo meetings held there.

There was another set of fingerprints on the stairwell near the office. They were light, and they hadn't been able to identify them yet.

"Let's talk to the housekeeper." Grasso said. "She'll know who's been in the house."

"Right after this." Ruiz gave her a thumbs up then continued moving through the report. "Look here— footprints found in the carpet downstairs." There was a photo attached.

"A men's size 8 shoe." Grasso read the note. "What's Winslow's size? Another question for the housekeeper."

Grasso finished her sandwich and balled up the plastic wrap.

She took aim at the trash can on the other side of the desk and made it easily.

"Jimmy, you were saying that talking to Daley had changed your thoughts about how to look at the invasions. What did you mean by that?"

"This is a crime that's easy to classify as a robbery gone bad." Ruiz leaned back in his chair, which protested with a creak. "But we need to look at all aspects of it. The robbery and the murder. If we're not getting anything that fits on the robbery end of it, let's look into the murder."

"Who hated Winslow and wanted him dead." Grasso rolled her eyes. "Besides everybody, I mean."

"Our last murder victim, Rosalind Mabrey, tried to do good things in the world. It's not as motivating to figure out who killed someone like Winslow, but we still gotta do it."

Grasso groaned. "The harassment case shows who he was. I'm just not that excited about finding—" She curled her fingers into air quotes "—the evil killer."

**9**

———

By 3 p.m., Ruiz had gotten hold of Olga Kostenko. She'd agreed to talk to them at her apartment in Redwood City. They got back into the Prius and headed north, this time taking 101 which was more direct.

Olga lived on the second floor of an apartment complex in East Redwood City. It was a faded stucco building, worse for wear on the outside, but when Olga invited them inside the small apartment, Grasso was pleased to see it was a bright, clean space. Intricately painted, colorful eggs—which she'd learned from a Ukrainian friend were called *pysanki*—were assembled on a display in the living room. A yellow and blue flag was pinned across an entire wall of the room.

A woman who looked to be about 80, sat bundled in a quilt, in a chair not far from a TV, where she rocked while watching Judge Judy.

Olga, a woman with graying blond hair, shrugged. "Worried about her? My mother can't understand a thing we say. She has dementia."

Grasso and Ruiz exchanged glances.

"That's fine." Ruiz nodded. "Olga, we want to ask you some questions about your employer, Derrick Winslow."

Olga tilted her head and looked sad. "I am sorry he is dead. He paid me so good. That's hard to find."

Olga spoke English well, though with a strong accent.

"When did you leave that night of the robbery and murder?" Ruiz asked.

"I always work Monday through Saturday, from 10 a.m. to 4 p.m. I clean, call for any services or appointments Mr. Winslow needs. I make his breakfast and lunch. That day— same. Nothing different. I left at 4, since I have to catch bus back to Redwood City to relieve my sister here. She works from 5 to midnight."

Grasso jumped in here. "Have you seen other people at the house?"

Olga smiled sweetly. "Of course. Mr. Winslow had many people over. Many beautiful ladies. And he also had meetings in his conference room and on the back deck. People would come by, and they would sit and do Zooms with the people in other countries."

"Were there some people who came over more often?" Grasso asked.

"Yes, Mr. Fisk. And a young man, Jeff—Mr. Gabbard. They were there to meet with Mr. Winslow many times. There were some ladies who came there often. Like a woman who was there last week. She had come many times before in the past month. Very beautiful but very lazy lady. That day, she slept until almost noon in Mr. Winslow's bedroom, and I couldn't start cleaning his room until 1. That messed me up and I couldn't clean till after lunch."

"Do you know her name?" Grasso asked. "Did you talk with her?"

Olga Kostenko gave them a wry look. "Oh, she would not

talk to *me*. To her, I was invisible. She looked like a model. With fat lips like a fish and a big ass. Long hair, you know, that she had to spend a lot of time curling in the bathroom before she left." Olga did a comical imitation of the woman frantically turning a curling iron in her hand over all sides of her head. Ruiz let out a hearty laugh.

"Did you hear her name, Olga?" he asked.

"When Mr. Winslow left that day, he told me that Miss Somebody might stay for lunch." Olga stopped to think. "Miss—with a B...*Becker*, I think."

"Olga, you left at 4 p.m. that day." Grasso jotted that down on her tablet. "Was Mr. Winslow there at the time? Did anyone else come over?"

Olga was quiet for a time, thinking. "He was there the whole time, working in his office upstairs. Nobody came. Nobody."

Her emphasis made Grasso suspicious. Who was she lying about?

"Did he mention anyone coming over later?"

Olga shook her head. "He didn't usually say anything to me. But people were always coming to his house. He was more happy when people were there."

Even Winslow didn't like himself, Grasso thought. Remembering the CSI report, she asked the woman. "By any chance, do you know Mr. Winslow's shoe size?"

"He wore a size ten." Olga responded immediately.

Ruiz leaned toward the woman, a serious look on his face.

"You've seen many people at your employer's house. Was there anyone you saw there who scared you?"

Olga sat up in her seat.

Her lip curled. She let out a puff of a laugh.

"Nobody scares me anymore, detective."

AFTER THE DETECTIVES LEFT, Olga Kostenko brought a glass of cold water with a straw to her mother. She held the glass and let her drink. Mama sucked, while watching the judge on TV with empty grey eyes. When the judge yelled or banged her wooden hammer, she got startled and stopped. It took a lot of nudging to get her mother to finish the entire glass.

Olga went to check her phone to see if she had any messages. Nothing. Things had moved fast over the past week, and she didn't want to miss anything. Each text she received could be an opportunity for money. Sometimes, to survive, it was not necessary to consider right and wrong. Only what is needed to live.

And that is why she responded to that last text, the day he was killed.

The two detectives were only trying to find out the truth. It had gotten very bad in the days before Winslow's death. She'd heard the phone calls, the threatening messages back and forth. Winslow wasn't a good man, true, but he had power, and sometimes you have to become good friends with people who have power. They can keep you safe.

The problem is, when they're dead, they cannot keep you safe.

Mr. Winslow paid her *not* to do things. It was that simple. To keep her head down and do her job. Keep cleaning and preparing meals with a smile. Make the phone calls you're asked to make. Don't tell about the ladies coming to the house, especially do not tell them about *each other*. And if you hear anything in a meeting or phone call here at the house—remember: you heard nothing.

She always kept her lips sealed. Smiled and said nothing.

That day last week, Winslow was on a phone call in his office, and she was making up the beds in the guest bedrooms across the hall. He was loud, probably because he had come to trust her and did not think of her as a presence in his house anymore. She was an appliance, like the refrigerator or stove.

That day, no one was expected until the GrowGo board members after she left, at 5 p.m.

He explained a plan. With many details that she did not understand. But she knew. This was a plan for death.

When the plan was put into action, a person would be destroyed.

So, when she received the text that day, she felt disloyal to Mr. Winslow. As if she'd broken the terms of their deal.

She knew that could be dangerous. But she texted back anyway.

**10**

———————

When they returned to the station, Ruiz and Grasso got to work trying to find the mystery woman who'd stayed at Winslow's house. They had only Olga's description to go on and her memory that the woman's last name was Becker.

They searched Facebook first. Derrick Winslow had a personal account, though after scrolling through it, they saw he hadn't posted much. Mostly he had been tagged by other people, with congratulations on successful startup sales. A photo of a cocktail party with attractive people mingling and drinking was labeled: HAPPY 52$^{nd}$, DERRICK!

"Let's take a look at his friends."

Ruiz clicked Derrick's friend list—10,708 total. They scrolled through the list, which took several minutes. There were a lot of women there, but none that seemed to match the description from Olga.

"You do know that most people on Facebook are over fifty, right?" Grasso said. "If she's young, she won't even be on Facebook. It's mostly older people these days."

"We could find some of Winslow's friends and ask them who the mystery woman is." Ruiz went back to the article he'd downloaded on Winslow. He remembered reading quotes from a friend in the article.

"I could see if there are any models locally who have the last name Becker." Grasso started searching on her phone.

After an hour, they had nothing. Ruiz reached the friend, Gordon Howell, another venture builder, who said he wasn't aware of who Winslow had "dated." He made a point of telling Ruiz he was putting quotes on the word *dated* as he said it, since Winslow's relationships tended to be a series of one-night stands and infatuations.

Grasso couldn't find any local models with the last name Becker, so she moved on. She searched YouTube for any videos or talks Derrick Winslow might have given. The problem with investigating a murder was you couldn't get to know the victim. You couldn't see them in action. Grasso wanted to see Derrick Winslow as a walking, talking human being. Maybe seeing that would help her be more motivated to solve his murder. And hopefully give her some understanding as to why people continued to work with—and date—the guy.

She found a few lectures by Winslow. A couple were pitches for GrowGo's venture building services. Others were talks on sales and marketing for startups.

She clicked on a sales pitch for GrowGo. After an intro of hip-sounding acoustic jazz, Derrick Winslow appeared, sitting in a familiar place—the deck of his Monte Verde home, a beautiful green backyard and forest of redwood trees behind him.

Derrick held a glass of red wine. The camera moved to a table nearby, where a group of good-looking twentysomethings wearing hoodies talked and gestured enthusiastically about some vague but really exciting "tech business solution."

*Business solutions are growing. Like a well-tended tree, a business concept can grow from a seedling to a mighty redwood. The future belongs to you—and GrowGo can get you there sooner than you think. With the support of the best sales, marketing, and development resources in the world.*

Derrick Winslow talked casually and reassuringly, with his legs crossed. He wore a pristine white polo shirt, and khaki pants—all of it certainly expensive. Impeccably tasteful.

He held his wine glass up and let the California sun sparkle through it, then looked at the camera, his head slightly angled, as if to say, *Consider working with me. You, too, can have this life.*

The man had charisma. He was engaging. Charming. Grasso could see how this guy could be very persuasive. He was a big contrast to Michael Fisk.

"Any results on Miss Becker yet?" Ruiz called over to her "C'mon, Grasso. You're good at stalking people."

Grasso snorted at him.

"I just watched a promo video for GrowGo Studios, featuring Winslow. What a guy. It helped to see him in action. He was a persuasive guy. And strangely—kind of good looking." She shivered at the fact that she'd even said that.

"Let me stop those thoughts before they go too far, Grasso." Ruiz raised any eyebrow then looked down at some notes he'd made. "I just found out something interesting from talking to Gordon Howell. Winslow has a son, Justin, from his marriage. After the divorce, Winslow claimed the kid wasn't his, and he refused to pay any kind of support for years. Didn't speak to the boy till he was twelve."

Grasso got up and moved toward Ruiz's desk.

"The kid—Justin Winslow—is a freshman down the road at Stanford."

**11**

———

After leaving the station for the day, Grasso decided to drive to the Grasso's Fine Foods Menlo Park location.

It was a couple of miles off course from her usual route between MVPD and Tom's to get to one of her family's stores, but for a good pickup dinner, it was the best option.

As she entered the doors, she breathed in the familiar smells—herbed rotisserie chickens and *osso bucco* roasting, fresh baked ciabatta, and cases stocked with imported cheeses. When she reached the deli section, she used a toothpick to spear herself a couple of olives and glob of fresh burrata. She closed her eyes and savored the nutty taste of the olives and the rich, creaminess of the cheese.

She filled her basket with rotisserie chicken, a pint of roasted potatoes, a salad greens mix and a bottle of pinot grigio.

She felt tired and didn't want to cook tonight. Tom had been doing more than his share, and she wanted to pitch in. Grasso's Menlo Park store was managed by her aunt Lidia, so she considered it a safe place. No awkward confrontations with Alex or Anthony here. *Whew.*

As she approached checkout, she saw Lidia talking to a checker and decided to give her a friendly wave. Lidia at first didn't seem to recognize her, but then came over when she was paying for her purchase and gave her a big hug. Lidia, her father's sister-in-law, had been bad about shunning her. She was a warm, friendly person by nature and kept forgetting she was supposed to do it.

"This is my niece, Daniela." She nodded to the checker, who kept a pleasant smile on her face as she ran the items across the scanner. "She is a policewoman. That big case—the company president who got killed at Rancho San Antonio?" Lidia nodded triumphantly. "She solved it."

"I'm a police *detective*, Lidia, and it was me *and* Detective Ruiz." Grasso smiled after the correction. "I haven't seen you since last fall at Unnon's party. How have you been? How's Christina? And Sam?"

"They're good. Christina and her boyfriend are now engaged. Heads up, the wedding will be in December so mark your calendar. And Sam has decided to go into the Navy when he graduates this June."

"Wonderful. Please give them my love, Lidia." She gave her aunt a side hug, grabbed her bag and turned to leave.

She was almost to the doors when she heard her aunt calling after her.

"I hear you have a boyfriend, Daniela," her aunt said excitedly. "We can't wait to meet him."

SHE'D *WANTED* her grandfather to tell the family he was okay with her being a police detective, so they'd all speak to her again.

The one thing she hadn't wanted him to tell the family, he'd told them.

Grasso parked in Tom's driveway. She got out and opened the back hatch of her car to get the bags. She was so tired, she didn't have the energy to be mad about Unnon spreading the news around the family. If Lidia knew about Tom, her parents would, too. She was surprised she hadn't gotten a call.

She opened the door from the garage into Tom's kitchen and dropped her bags on the marble island. Then she screwed off the top of the pinot grigio and poured herself a glass. No corkscrew needed. There was nothing like easy access.

Tom came up behind her and kissed her neck.

"You brought dinner," he said, close to her ear and it turned her thoughts away from her family troubles. A ripple of warm electricity ran through her.

He had his arms around her, and she let herself lean back into him, feeling his sweater against her and the warmth of his body through it.

"You got all the good stuff." He held her close. "Let's take the wine to the couch." She nodded. She felt like she was going to cry, but nothing was coming out.

He grabbed the bottle and they headed for the living room couch, where much of their life took place.

"We're having dinner at Unnon's on Thursday. That still okay?"

"Of course." He studied her face with an amused smile. "I'm looking forward to it."

She turned and looked at him. "Really? Even though my family is completely fucked up?"

"Dani, I don't have a history with your family. It doesn't affect me like it does you."

She took a gulp of her wine. "Unnon told everybody in the family you and I were coming over. And that this was the big boyfriend announcement."

"I feel special—I'm going to sit back and enjoy all the attention." Tom said with a wry smile. "I'm being realistic. There are a lot of things they might not like about me. I'm older than you. By a lot. I'm not even a little bit Italian. Working for a grocery store is the last thing I'd want to do with my life. But I want to meet them because they're the people who made you. And they did a great job."

She sunk her face into his chest and breathed in the freshly washed smell of his sweater, his musky skin, and the menthol scent of eucalyptus trees he'd picked up from his backyard.

"Why are you not taken? Why do I get to be with you?" she said, her voice choked with emotion she couldn't fully express.

He looked down at her with that twisted smile he got when he was trying hard not to smile. It got her every time.

"I didn't understand work-life balance until last year. That's why."He kissed the top of her head. "You lucky girl. You came along at just the right time."

After dinner, they sat next to each other on the couch, game controllers in hand as they faced the PlayStation console. They'd spent almost a half an hour outfitting their avatars with flashy armor and weaponry. Tom had just bought his avatar a helmet that looked a cross between a drum major's hat and a bushel of wheat. Every time Tom made his character spin around and show it off, she laughed.

"Where should we head to?" Tom made his character

jump up and down on the screen amid the landscape of sand, rocks, and red jagged mountains in the distance.

"Toward the canyon," Grasso commanded, making her character veer in the direction of the shadowy rock formation on the right side of the screen. "And hopefully some treasure."

"That seems too obvious." Tom's character followed hers across the sand. "Would not be surprised to run into a pack of *zigar* worms when we get there."

"Yeah. But *zigar* worms are cannon fodder," she said, almost impatiently, her eyes on the screen. "Between the two of us, we can take them."

"Fine. But be warned." Tom followed Grasso into the canyon, where all light seemed to disappear. They were now in a lush, dark place, lit by phosphorescent pinkish clouds hanging low over the canyon. Waterfalls trickled down from the canyon walls, sparks flashing in the water as it fell.

"This is a beautiful place." Tom leaped back and forth over a narrow creek. "Surely *nothing* bad can happen to us here."

Grasso flashed him an amused look. "Let's find that treasure."

They explored for a while, till they came to a few *zigar* worms, who popped up from behind a tree stump.

"Crossbow!" Grasso called to Tom.

"Got 'em," Tom said calmly, while Dani cheered. A few arrows and the *zigar* flared up in a poof of pink smoke, leaving behind its shell and piles of gold tokens, which Tom quickly picked up. "Let's keep moving toward the other side of the canyon. There might be a chest."

They had to jump over fallen logs and rock formations, so it took them a while to get to the other side, where a red light gleamed on the other side of a huge rockpile.

"We're blocked in," Grasso moaned. "We'll have to back out."

Suddenly a towering prehistoric creature, like a T-rex but much, much bigger, lumbered into view.

"Holy shit." Tom backed his character up.

"Let's try coming up right beneath him and see if that works." Dani pushed forward, until her character was standing right in front of the Boss—this enormous creature they had to defeat in order to win the campaign.

She started using her mace on the creature's legs, while Tom began shooting his crossbow, with fire power on his arrows. His attack barely affected the creature, who quickly destroyed them both with one belch of his fire breath.

Soon the weird, orange-tentacled non-player character (NPC) hovered over the screen, echoing his annoying catchphrase:

*We shall return to fight as partners ere the suns of Azir rise.*

Grasso groaned and flopped down on the couch. "Oh, my God. It's frustrating enough to lose our campaign without having that guy pop up to say that *every fricking time*. I am so sick of him."

"Really?" Tom lay back on the couch, his arms behind his head. "You've never mentioned it."

When Tom laughed, she threw a pillow at him.

# 12

On his way in to the SJPD homicide pit with his coffee and croissant, Mario Flores passed Mandy Dirkson, on the phone at her desk. She checked him out for a good five seconds, then rolled her eyes and looked away.

"Good morning, Mandy." He nodded and gave her what he hoped was a pleasant smile. She ignored him.

She'd been part of his team—a group of detectives he'd led who'd worked together well, had a great sense of camaraderie, got together outside of the job, and had a high clearance rate for cases. But it had been a year since he'd crashed and burned in the department. A year since Mandy had called and told Ruiz that Flores had been having an affair with his wife.

Today he had his chance to change that. At ten, he'd meet with Sergeant Buckley.

His performance under Buckley's leadership had been good, even though Flores had picked up a bad habit of grinding his teeth at night. Flores had just closed the Lopez grocery case and had discovered a connection with another downtown murder-robbery six months ago. An arrest with two murder charges, and downtown felt a little safer now.

With Jesperson, he felt like he was always running a little faster than the supervisor wanted him to, chasing after leads that his by-the-book supervisor didn't understand—making the man nervous and suspicious. But Flores had learned to be patient. He took the time to explain the steps in his reasoning to Jesperson—and Eric Roberson, the detective he'd been paired up with on the Lopez grocery case. Covered his ass with meticulous paperwork, something that came easy to him. He wanted Buckley to know he was doing everything right. That he was committed to the job.

And that he wanted back in.

At ten, he went into Buckley's office. The sergeant was on the phone, a slight smile on his face, responding to someone with a lot of *yeahs* and *sures*. Finally, he finished off with a *you got it*. And a very kiss-uppy *no, thank* you.

He looked up at Flores in surprise. Then he shuffled a pile on his desk, as if looking for something he'd misplaced.

"I forgot we were meeting." He pushed a button on his phone and took off his reading glasses. "Let's make this quick."

"I'd like to be considered as a team leader." He put it out there, short and sweet. "It's been a year."

Buckley looked distracted, still patting his desk to find something and glancing to the door. "Has it? Since—oh, yeah, the Schuler case."

"I've made mistakes in the past, I know that. But I've shown what I can do. Look at the Lopez grocery store murder and the connected case downtown, with Roberson and me. I want the chance to lead the team again." Now he added the lie. "I've learned a lot from my time with Jesperson."

Buckley started laughing. "Don't bullshit me. I know you and Jesperson are polar opposites. Flores, c'mon. Your team had a high close rate on some difficult cases. You did a good job on the downtown grocery case. But I need to be able to trust my detectives. I couldn't trust you. And I've heard the gossip."

Sweat began to dampen the back of his shirt. Flores took a deep breath. "You can trust me now. Believe me."

Buckley had a faint smile on his face. "We'll see. I've got to run to a meeting. Let's revisit this when I have more time. A week from today. Same time."

With that, Buckley got up, grabbed a folder off his desk and left.

A hot wave of anger rose up in Flores's chest.

He thought of all he'd done this past year to change, to up his game. All the taunting he'd received from his fellow detectives, and the sucking up he'd done with Jesperson. He had been working on his pitch all week. This morning he'd laid out all his hopes, dreams, and pride before Buckley.

And the sergeant had just walked out.

"YOU TAKE the lead in interviewing the kid," Ruiz said as they drove down the palm-tree-lined boulevard into Stanford University.

"With you, it'll be like he's talking to a fellow freshman." He shot her a grin.

"I have a few years before I'll appreciate that as a

compliment," Grasso said. "But I think you're right. He may respond better to someone younger."

"We don't know much about him." Ruiz turned onto Campus Drive. "Could he have killed his father? He's nineteen. But when you think about it, males between eighteen and twenty-four are the most likely group to engage in gun violence. Not that it justifies it, but he *had* a reason; his dad refused to accept him as his kid."

"I only had that short term." Grasso said quietly, and Ruiz regretted that he'd brought up being disowned. "I had enough of it to know it doesn't feel good."

"His father did finally acknowledge him," Ruiz said, as he turned off Mayfield Avenue into a parking lot near Tressider Student Union. Ruiz had been here before but was always impressed after a walk through the campus, with its lush green quads, sculptures, and beautiful old buildings. "Maybe the two of them ended up connecting and becoming close."

Grasso gave him a *Who Even Are You?* look.

"I can't believe you're saying that unironically, Jimmy. We know what kind of guy his dad was. What do you think the chances are that they ever had a cozy, loving relationship?"

Ruiz shrugged as he parked. "Stranger things have happened." If marriages could be repaired, as he saw the smallest signs of happening between him and Reyna, maybe a father and son relationship could be fixed. Sometimes he was afraid that if you stopped hoping for things, they would never happen. Like he remembered hearing some verse from the bible in Sunday school about how Jesus couldn't perform a miracle in a town that had no faith. You had to hold on to it to get your miracle—holding on like it was a rope, dangling over a dark chasm.

They walked to the outdoor tables behind the student union where they'd agreed to meet Justin Winslow. Students had ventured outdoors when the sun had come out today, so many of the tables were filled with students studying or just meeting up between classes. The dress code for the still-chilly day seemed to include shorts and expensive sunglasses.

Ruiz scanned the tables and saw a skinny, dark-haired kid, sitting by himself at a far table reading a book. Every once in a while, the kid looked up and swiveled his head around to look for someone. Ruiz remembered the photo of Derrick Winslow on the cover of the magazine. This kid had his face, his hair. Ruiz felt sorry for him because of it. Justin had his look, but even at a distance, it was obvious that he had a different personality.

"He looks so alone," said Grasso. "That's got to be him."

"Justin Winslow?" She smiled warmly as they came to his table. "I'm Detective Dani Grasso. This is Detective Jimmy Ruiz."

The kid nodded and shut the thick book, which was called *Buddenbrooks*. Ruiz hadn't heard of the book but guessed his major wasn't computer engineering.

Justin Winslow stood up stiffly and shook both their hands, then sat down. There was a look of fear on his face. His skinny frame trembled under his red Stanford t-shirt.

"You reading that for a class?" Grasso asked as they sat down. Ruiz sat back and watched the kid. And the brazen little birds that frequently fluttered down to the tables to look for food.

"Twentieth Century Literature," Justin Winslow said, with a tilt of his head. "There's a lot of reading in the class. Someday, I'm going to be a writer. I'm going to write about truth."

"We wanted to talk to you about your father." Grasso watched for his reaction. "I'm sorry for your loss."

The kid's lip turned up in disgust.

"For me it wasn't a loss. It was a relief." Justin spat out the words. "And don't call him my father. The only thing he ever did for me as a father was to pay for me to come here."

"Sorry to hear that, Justin," Grasso continued sympathetically.

"I heard that your father was not a part of your life until you were twelve. Is that right?"

Justin nodded. "My mom divorced him when I was two. She fought to get support for me, but the fuckwit wouldn't admit I was his son, even though they were *married*. Even after a paternity test, he wouldn't admit it. He didn't start paying until I was in middle school because my mom finally hired a lawyer and he had to. He thought I was going to take all his money away."

Grasso looked over at Ruiz. Another confirmation of the most important thing in Derrick Winslow's life.

"Where did you and your mom live, Justin? Around here?"

"We lived in Monte Verde, up in the hills. Not far from where Fuckwit lived. A few blocks away and he still couldn't make time to see me."

Ruiz thought about the wounds Winslow had inflicted on his son by rejecting him. How hurtful it must have been to know he had a father so close by, yet his father was not giving him what he knew a father should give. His own situation, with an abusive father who eventually left, had been different, but Ruiz understood how conflicted a kid's views on a father could be.

Ruiz also wondered if Justin had heard of the Millers. He would have been thirteen at the time. Maybe he was one of those kids who'd spread the neighborhood legend of the home invasion and the family's tragic deaths. He might have known the details of the murders.

Now he heard Grasso building bridges with the kid, as someone who lived in the Monte Verde hills.

"Hey, no way," Grasso said, with the nonchalant voice of a seen-it-all teen. "I live on Laurelwood Road. What street were you on?"

"Folsom," the kid said, a suspicious look in his eyes.

Ruiz's heart sped up. Justin Winslow must have heard of the murders five years ago. He may have known Christopher Miller. He seemed like a smart kid, too. Could he have dreamed up a clever way to kill the father he hated—by making it appear to be a home invasion?

"I've got some questions," Grasso said, continuing with her nonchalant, almost-a-teen voice. She shrugged. "'Cause we gotta ask everybody, right? Where were you the night of the murder?"

Justin bristled, as much as someone who was also very afraid could bristle.

"I was in my dorm room. I'm taking Calculus because my mom made me. She wants me to go into tech. I hate it. I had a test the next morning."

"You have any roommates, Justin?"

He slunk down on the bench and looked back at her sullenly. "I'm in a single room."

"You didn't leave the dorm?"

"I was there all night."

"Anybody you might have talked to that evening?"

"The RA on my floor, Michael Kim. He said 'hi' to me on the way to the bathroom. Does that count?"

Grasso shrugged in an offhand way. "Sure. I guess it does."

Grasso wished the kid the best of luck with his semester, and they said goodbye. The kid opened his thick book and continued reading.

When they were a few yards away, Ruiz looked back at the kid.

He was watching them leave.

**13**

———

They drove on Campus Drive out of Stanford. In the nearby fields, soccer players chased a ball. A line of cyclists wearing backpacks zipped down the path next to them on their way out of campus.

At the stop sign before El Camino, Ruiz beat his hands on the steering wheel.

"We need to check his alibi with the RA and find out exactly when he talked to him. I doubt the kid spent the whole night in his room with only one bathroom break." Ruiz shot a look at Grasso, who was looking something up on her phone. "Justin Winslow grew up a block away from the Millers. He would have known about the robbery and murders."

"So, you think this kid staged a home invasion?" Grasso's voice was calmer than she felt.

"He's pissed off and he seems smart." Ruiz turned onto El Camino to head for the Page Mill entrance to 280. "And he looks just like his dad. I could picture him shooting his father in the face, maybe for that reason."

Grasso didn't seem as excited about this prospect as he would have liked.

"He's only 19," she said, looking out the passenger side window. "He's probably been angry at his dad all his life. It's a full-time job for him. What would have made him snap *this* week?"

Ruiz was about to say maybe Derrick Winslow had threatened to cut his son off. Then he remembered that the kid had said the *only* good thing his dad had done was to pay for his education.

"Let's talk to the mother," Ruiz said as they turned onto Page Mill. "I'm sure she's got an interesting perspective on Winslow—and Justin."

BACK AT THE STATION, Ruiz tried to contact the dorm resident advisor, Michael Kim, and Grasso called Marcia Winslow Davies, Justin's mother.

Rather than talk over the phone, Grasso asked her to come by the station. She was now living in Palo Alto, and it wasn't far away. She'd rather have them meet the woman in person. She suspected and hoped they'd have a long conversation.

At 3 p.m., Grasso went out to buzz her in. The woman sat in the waiting room scrolling through her phone. She was a nicely dressed woman, probably in her late forties, an expensive scarf draped around her neck.

Grasso put her head out the door.

"Come on back, Mrs. Davies." The woman stood up, gave her a tight, professional-looking smile, and followed her in.

She sat on the side of the table next to Mrs. Davies, and Ruiz sat across from them.

"Would you like some coffee, Mrs. Davies?" Ruiz offered. "The coffee's actually good here."

The woman smiled genuinely. "Thank you. It's been a long day."

While Ruiz retrieved the coffee, Grasso tried to establish a rapport with Justin's mother.

"We talked to Justin today," Grasso said with a smile. "That must be nice to have him at a school so close by."

A worried look crossed the woman's pretty face. "I hope he didn't get too upset. His feelings for his father are...complicated."

Grasso nodded sympathetically, as Ruiz brought in one of the fancy mugs with coffee for Mrs. Davies.

"Mrs. Davies, we asked you to come in to answer some questions about your ex-husband." Ruiz said as he took a seat opposite. "And your son."

The woman pursed her lips and her look darkened.

"I didn't have much to do with Derrick after the divorce. He wanted it that way. He refused to talk to me, and he would not acknowledge Justin as his biological son."

Ruiz acted like this was news to him. "Is there some reason why he wouldn't, Mrs. Davies?"

The woman's face crumpled. She pulled a tissue from her purse and wiped her nose. "It started out so well, our marriage. Derrick was an extrovert, the life of any gathering. He could be very charming. We were only engaged for a couple of months, then we got married on impulse in Paris —which was his idea. When we came back to the US, I found out I was pregnant. All of the sudden Derrick turned into a different person. He became obsessed with money. I realized I'd made a big mistake. I hadn't known him at all.

He obsessed about our finances and demanded I quit pursuing my degree and get a job."

"What did you do?" Grasso realized they were getting good insight into who their murder victim was, even though it was depressing as hell.

Marcia Winslow Davies took a deep breath, blotted her nose, and continued.

"I told him I wanted a divorce, that I'd married him in the heat of the moment and hadn't realized what I was getting into. Derrick said he wouldn't pay child support. He wasn't going to have a child drain all his money. Especially if it wasn't *his*—according to him. Derrick had a way of putting a little dig in everything. Implying nasty things without coming out and saying it. He did it with a smile. It was incredibly painful." She bit her lip.

Grasso glanced at Ruiz. They were getting an up close and personal description of who Derrick Winslow was. They'd let her keep talking.

"I found out talking to some of Derrick's college friends that he'd always had issues with money, always obsessed that he didn't have enough. His father left him and his mom when he was five, and they lived as one of the few poor families in a wealthy suburb. He felt singled out at school, the one kid who got a free lunch. To him, not having money was like not having power. He made sure he'd never be like that again. I'm not saying that justifies his behavior, but it's helped me to understand him."

Grasso just shook her head. Wow.

"When Justin was diagnosed with autism at the age of six, that made it worse. When I continued to ask for support, Derrick claimed that he hadn't fathered Justin. And further proof of it was that autism didn't run in *his* family."

"Oh my God," Grasso said almost involuntarily. She

wanted to slap the table. She willed herself to be calm. She took a deep breath and tried to recover. "So, Justin said something about a paternity test."

"The paternity test showed that Justin was Derrick's son. No question."

Was it worth it? Grasso wondered if it would have been better to have lied and told Derrick Winslow that Justin wasn't his son and cut all ties with her ex. That way Justin wouldn't have the knowledge that Fuckwit was his dad.

"It took how long for him to finally pay you child support?" Ruiz asked.

"Six years." Marcia Davies enunciated the words clearly. "I was busy building my career, and I should have done it sooner. I finally retained a lawyer. That didn't help Justin much. Derrick only began to have visits with him when Justin was twelve. Those were miserable for him. Thankfully I remarried a man who became like a father to him. Kenneth's been great."

"Did you have any contact with your son the night of Derrick's murder?" Ruiz asked. The woman got a scared look on her face.

"I called his cell to check in on him. He was studying for a Calculus test and said he had a lot to make up."

"Mrs. Davies, where were you the night Derrick Winslow was killed?" Ruiz casually slid the question right in there, and it had an immediate effect on the woman.

"But you don't think that I would—" The woman swallowed. "I was home, preparing a talk for a data management conference this weekend up in Berkeley. Kenneth can vouch for me. I didn't hear about Derrick's death till I listened to the local news the next morning."

"The way you and your son were treated, it makes sense that you'd be angry with your ex-husband." Ruiz leaned back in his chair, a sympathetic look on his face. "Are you still angry at him?"

Marcia Winslow Davies froze in place for a minute or two. The question hadn't released a flood of anger. She looked as though she didn't understand the question. Or it had completely stumped her.

Ruiz glanced at Grasso, as they waited for the woman to answer.

"I—I don't know. I've spent years trying to shield Justin from his dad. Worried about how his father's attitude would hurt him. I've obsessed about it. I've been so angry at Derrick on Justin's behalf." In contrast with her words, her voice was calm and thoughtful. "I'm honestly not sure how *I* feel about him. He was selfish. Despicable. So, yes. I think I did hate him. But I also felt sorry for him. For whatever kept him so fixated on money, to the exclusion of the people in his life."

"Another question, Mrs. Davies," Ruiz began. "This may sound random, but did you once live on Folsom Road, here in Monte Verde?"

A shadow passed over Marcia Winslow Davies' face.

"Justin and I lived in a house there for a couple of years before I married Kenneth. About six years ago."

Ruiz almost beamed, a look Grasso thought of as Ruiz's *nothing going on here. Just asking* face.

"We appreciate you coming to the station today, Mrs. Davies. If you can think of anything about Justin or your ex-husband that would be helpful for us to know, please give Detective Grasso or me a call."

"THAT MAN INFURIATES ME." Grasso let out a growl. "What a selfish asshole. Winslow refused to accept his son because he was diagnosed with autism, and it didn't run in *his* family."

"I noticed you got upset when Mrs. Davies said that." Ruiz studied her face. "I was wondering why."

Grasso brushed the hair off her forehead. "It's my nephew, Alex's son, Arlo. He's being evaluated for autism. I've been thinking about him lately. He's such a cool kid. The thought of anyone thinking of him as unacceptable just pisses me off."

Ruiz put his hands behind his head and leaned back in his chair to stretch. "We have to call this one. Enough people hated Derrick Winslow, so there's no shortage of suspects. Was it a murder made to look like a robbery gone bad?"

"Justin and his mom were right down the street from the Millers five years ago." Grasso leaned her head on one arm. "It would have been a huge deal that this happened a few blocks away. Maybe she was friends with Jennie Miller. As a 13-year-old in the neighborhood, Justin would probably know the gory details."

"Coincidences do happen," Ruiz pushed his chair back and stood up. "But we need evidence. Still hoping for Crime Scene to give us more on that last set of unidentified fingerprints. And I talked to computer forensics. They'll check Winslow's computers for emails or texts from anyone he might have met with that day or night."

"I'm still trying to find the mystery woman Olga Kostenko was talking about. I'm not sure I have enough info to find her."

"Touch base if you find anything. I gotta cut out a little early today for marriage counseling."

"So, it's going okay?" Grasso heard skepticism in her own voice. She wanted everything to improve between Jimmy and Reyna. Every week, she'd see either grouchy Ruiz or walking-on-air Ruiz, depending on how things went in the session. The man was a clean glass window when it came to feelings.

Ruiz didn't say a lot about how the sessions went, though sometimes he'd mention some realization he'd come to after their session. Grasso hoped Reyna was also having some realizations.

Ruiz grunted. "It's a lot of ups and downs."

He wasn't going to share much. He'd chosen to stay with Reyna after the affair and after she'd bluntly told him she didn't love him. It wasn't what *she'd* do in that situation, but Grasso knew Ruiz hadn't made his decision lightly, and apparently Reyna had been open to counseling.

She still prayed to St. Jude for him, while hoping St. Jude was okay with the fact that she was sleeping with her boyfriend.

As far as she was concerned, Ruiz's marriage was still a lost cause.

**14**

———

The opportunity had dropped into Flores' lap. Jesperson was out for three days—left early for a fishing trip with his buddies up in the Delta near Sacramento.

At 1:30 p.m., a call came in about a body found in a motel room near the airport.

Flores poked his head into Buckley's office to ask if he and Roberson could go check it out. The two of them had a reputation for taking turns as the butt monkeys *de jour*, always free and a little too eager to take work on.

As they drove over, Eric Roberson was as excited as he was. The rookie started doing a little dance in place with hand motions as they followed highway 87 up toward the airport.

They arrived at the motel, which Flores would peg as a one-star accommodation, maybe one-half star. It looked like it had been built in the 1970s, Flores judged by the blue and white, beach-themed architecture. The white railings on the walkway were decorated with stylized blue dolphins.

He pulled up next to the patrol officer's car. Officer Kate

Carrera led them to the scene: a room on the second floor, where a young woman lay on her back on the bathroom floor in a pool of blood. She looked young—maybe underage—and Hispanic, with long, dark shiny hair. She wore only a t-shirt and pink underwear with a cartoon character on it. She'd been shot in the stomach and the chest.

At the sight of the young woman, he and Roberson suddenly sobered up and slipped on gloves.

"The housekeeper found her when she opened the room to clean," said Carrera, a stocky officer with short blond hair. "The desk says the room was registered to a Ronald J. Perez, of Long Beach, California. He checked out at noon."

The guy could go a long distance in two hours.

"They record a license plate?"

Carrera gave him a grim look. "*Nuh-uh*. They said they don't do that here."

"No make and model of car?"

Flores searched the room for a purse or any identification for the young woman. In the drawer on top of Gideon's Bible, there was a small, flat wallet, made of slick, brightly colored duct tape. He recognized it right away, since his sister Dawn used to make them and sell them to her friends as a pre-teen.

He looked through the cards. A VTA card for riding the bus in Santa Clara Valley. A photo of a younger girl who looked about five. Then a high school ID card, with a bashful, smiling photo of the girl now on the floor in the bathroom. It said she was a sophomore as of this school year.

Ana Fuentes.

"Found something?" Carrera came around to look at the photo. "*Jesus.* She's underage by three years."

*Ana, what's your story?*

Flores looked at the photo of the girl as if he could read her face to see what fate she'd been headed for at the time her photo was taken. Trafficking. Or prostitution. Maybe she'd run away from a shitty home situation with someone—this Ronald Perez—somebody she thought could help her get out.

"Roberson," he called to the rookie, who was poking through items in the bathroom and taking photos of the girl's body from different angles with a department camera.

"Go to the motel desk and ask if anyone there remembers anything about Ronald Perez's car in Room 2D —make or model. If nobody does, find out who was working last night when they checked in. Get their number and ask them."

Flores took out his cell phone. He didn't know if she'd answer, or if she'd want to do anything for him. But she was the best and fastest at it.

He called Mandy Dirkson's cell number.

Four rings. Then it rolled over to voice mail. He left his message.

"Mandy, I know you despise me, but please do this for me. I'm at Ocean Shore Motel with a murder victim, a minor, in a suspected trafficking situation. Do a search for Ronald J. Perez, 1423 Wake Street in Long Beach. Roberson and I need priors and vehicle info."

He continued searching the room. There was a lot the housekeeper missed. A plastic fork with what looked like salsa or spaghetti sauce on it, stuck to the carpet near the nightstand. Under the bed he found a menu for a Mexican restaurant nearby. It was torn in two. He picked up the pieces, then saw something scrawled on the other side. He put the pieces together and saw it, as tears stung his eyes.

> HELP
> 911
> ROOM 2D

Maybe she'd been caught trying to get someone's attention and had been shot. Maybe she'd tried to get away. The words were scrawled with a ball point pen. They probably could not have been read from very far if the girl had held them up to the window.

"Oh my God." Carrera said as she read it. "That motherfucker."

They could hear Roberson running up the stairs. He came in the open door.

"He's driving a Blue Chevy Cruz."

A minute or two later, Roberson's phone rang, a jingle that sounded like the Doctor Who theme song.

"Yeah? Give me the plate number, Mandy." Roberson did a little jig around the room, patting the bureau and opening nightstands looking for a pen and paper.

"Just say it and we'll write it down!" Carrera barked out.

Roberson did that, and both she and Flores typed it into their phones.

Mandy wouldn't call him back, but she'd called Roberson and that was enough. With the plate number, make and model, Ronald J. Perez would be apprehended and arrested an hour later on Highway 101, south of King City in the Central Valley for human trafficking and murder.

After the medical examiner finished and Ana Fuentes

was taken away, he and Roberson walked out of the stale air of the motel room into the fading light of the day.

He, Carrera, Roberson, and even Mandy had worked as a team to do the last thing they could to help 15-year-old Ana Fuentes. Flores was angry that they hadn't saved the girl, but when he heard Perez had been arrested, he felt a surge of relief and satisfaction. It did not matter now that Buckley hadn't noticed his hard work on the downtown case. He didn't fucking care.

The adrenaline would keep him awake most of the night.

THE LIGHTING in the counseling room was slightly dim. A fountain in the corner made a constant trickling sound.

Ruiz had to be careful not to drink too much water before they arrived. Hearing that damn fountain made him have to take a mid-session pee break every time.

Today, Reyna was talking about her feelings about parenting Jacky with him. When she talked first, it always made him nervous. As soon as she finished—and sometimes Reyna said some very painful things—Jennifer de Groot, LMFT, would turn to Ruiz and ask, "Jimmy, now how do *you* feel about what Reyna's saying?"

This is how he felt: naked, unprotected. Like he was standing in front of the wall waiting for the firing squad to shoot. He wasn't sure if what he said in response would hurt her or make her mad. But as they continued with the sessions, he realized another thing. Reyna did not speak up about these things *unless* they were in counseling. He'd rather hear them even if it hurt. If she actually said what she was thinking, they could talk about it. Which they'd been doing a lot more of lately.

"Thank you for saying you couldn't wish for a better father for Jacky. I can be overprotective with him sometimes."

"I feel like you don't trust me to make the right decisions with Jacky. Like you don't think I can keep him safe."

Ruiz rubbed his face. "Oh, God, Reyna. I trust you. But I'm a cop. I am always looking for potential dangers. I want to protect Jacky from the things I saw growing up. When he almost got shot last year on Benton, I felt like I'd failed to protect him."

Reyna started crying, then he felt tears in his eyes. God, he hated crying in front of people. Every week he went in knowing he was going to be stripped down, challenged, and pushed, made to scrutinize his own actions. He usually cried or said something stupid. Insensitive.

Jacky was one of the easiest topics to discuss. They both would do anything to keep him happy and safe.

"Reyna and Jimmy, you love Jacky, it's clear. This has gone well. I'm proud of you both. You have your homework for next time. Next week we'll be talking about something that might be more difficult." Ruiz tried to keep himself from groaning. "Your *physical* relationship."

Reyna hugged Jennifer when they left. He didn't feel like it, but the counselor always hugged Reyna, and when she asked him if he was okay with being hugged, he nodded. He felt he'd look like a dick if he didn't.

He and Reyna walked to their car in the parking lot in the dark, and for once it didn't feel like Reyna was hurrying to get home, or to pull out her phone to scroll through social media.

He was quiet as they walked side by side, hoping he was reading her right. She seemed softer tonight, less uptight.

As they approached the truck, he asked it.

"Would you be up for some dinner?"

"You know Colin would love to hang out with Jacky a little longer. They're probably playing Minecraft anyway." She laughed.

"Of course, they're playing Minecraft," he snorted. "Whenever we show up, they're going to say it's too soon."

Reyna turned to him, a slight smile on her face. "Yes, let's do dinner."

They drove to a Mexican place with good drinks. There were heaters on the patio, so they enjoyed dinner outside and had strong mojitos that made them just a little tipsy.

Ruiz told Reyna what he could about the Winslow case, and then a little about Grasso's brothers and their attempt to force her to introduce her parents to Tom.

"She should just do it. Ignore them and show no fear. They're obviously trying to get to her," Reyna said, as she took another sip of her second mojito. Her brown skin glowed in the candlelight; her eyes snapped. She was fire— moving, burning, flickering. She raised her hand to emphasize her words as she spoke. "Grasso should *not* give them the reaction they want."

Ruiz opened his eyes wide. He laughed. "Absolutely. That's what I told her."

They drove back talking about Jacky, remembering some of the crazy things he did as a toddler. Then talked about everything that went wrong at their wedding in Tahoe ten years ago and ended up laughing about it. A friend of his mother's had made a layered wedding cake but as soon as she set it on a plate, the top layer slid off. Later they'd locked themselves out of their honeymoon suite and had to sit on the floor outside of the room talking for a half-hour until someone came to let them back in.

They finally pulled up in front of Colin's house.

He wasn't sure, maybe it was the alcohol. Reyna turned toward him. When she put her hand on his, he almost stopped breathing.

"When he gets in the car, this will be over," she said.

When he spoke, his voice sounded hoarse.

"Doesn't mean we can't do it again."

THE NEXT MORNING, Ruiz woke up feeling light, with a kind of feathery feeling in his chest.

Reyna left for her spin class, so he rolled over and took up the whole bed. He slept in for another couple of snoozes on the alarm.

"Dad, are you going to take me to school or not?" Jacky appeared at the bedroom door. "You didn't come to wake me up."

"I never sleep in. I just felt like it today." He rubbed his eyes and smiled at the boy. The boy looked back at him, stunned by this response.

"That's weird." Jacky frowned, unsure of how to react to that. "You going to walk me to school or not?"

"You know I love to do that, *mijo*. I'll get up now. You get dressed and ready. Or we could play football." It was a game they'd played before Jacky started kindergarten.

Jacky eyes widened. He leaped up onto the bed, trying to grab the pink oval throw pillow on the bed that they used to call the "football."

Ruiz put the football down in the middle of the bed. Jacky waited at the foot of the bed, and Ruiz knelt at the head of the bed. They charged each other, and then ended up in a tackle in the middle of the bed, as Jacky jumped on his back to try to pull the pillow out from under him.

Jacky had declared a few years ago that tickling was an illegal move, but Ruiz did it anyway now, leaving Jacky clutching his side, dissolved in giggles in the middle of the bed, while Ruiz rolled off the end of the bed goal line with the "football."

"Hey, that's no fair!" Jacky recovered from the giggle fit and pounced on him on the floor, finally pulling the pillow away triumphantly.

"Winner!" Jacky jumped onto the bed, holding each end of the football high above his head.

The ringtone from Ruiz's cell phone began jangling on the nightstand.

"Jacky, bring me my phone," he called from the floor.

The boy stopped his victory dance and jumped off the bed to grab the phone.

"It's Dani," Jacky said, his eyes bright and his cheeks pink from the exercise. "Can I say hi?"

"Hand it to me, *mijo*." Ruiz stood up and took the phone. "Go get dressed and ready. We need to leave soon."

He answered. Grasso sounded different—serious, her early-morning perkiness subdued.

"Ruiz, I'm at the station early today after my run. We just got a report back from computer forensics. You need to come in and see this for yourself."

**15**

———

R uiz pulled into his spot in the back lot at MVPD. Five minutes late, but between sleeping in and football with Jacky, that wasn't bad.

Once inside, he passed Ladera's desk quickly, hoping not to have to engage in conversation. He saw Ladera look up at him sadly but moved on to the interrogation room where Grasso sat, documents laid out before her.

He nodded at Grasso and sat down across from her.

"What do we have?"

"Forensics looked at Winslow's wi-fi and generated a report for the 24-hour period from 8 am the morning of his murder to the following morning." She passed the printout to him. "See who logged on."

He looked at the names.

Olga Kostenko 10:15 a.m.-3:58 p.m.
Kira Baker 00:01 a.m.-1:30 p.m.
Jeffrey Gabbard 2:12-4:05 p.m.
Justin Winslow [username: Joker] 10:15-11:19 p.m.

"What the hell." Ruiz sighed and looked across at Grasso. "That's what we needed. Let's bring him in."

They took the Prius and cut across town to take El Camino Real to Stanford, then they followed the route onto campus they'd taken before. Grasso was quiet on the drive. He didn't feel the shared excitement they'd experienced in previous cases, of closing in on the case, the countdown to an arrest.

This time they parked near the on-campus housing, next to Justin Winslow's dorm.

Before he got out, Ruiz felt for the gun in his holster under his jacket. He nodded at Grasso, and they got out, making their way to the building entrance.

Rather than take the elevator, they chose the stairs. Grasso bounded up the four flights, but he was winded by the time they came to Justin's door.

Ruiz rapped on the door right under Justin's name. Below it was a picture clipped from a magazine of Heath Ledger as The Joker, lipstick smeared into a smile.

As they stood there, a group of students down the hall froze in place, fear in their eyes. Grasso waved them back.

"Justin Winslow." Ruiz called loudly, close to the door. "Open up. Monte Verde Police."

They waited. Ruiz had his hand near his holster, ready to spring into action if it turned out Justin Winslow would be part of the grim statistics for eighteen-to-twenty-four-year-old males. Grasso stood slightly to the side and farther back, her hand near her weapon.

Ruiz heard footsteps inside. Grasso tensed up and moved her hand to her gun. Ruiz rapped again, harder.

After about thirty seconds, the door opened. Justin Winslow stood in a white bathrobe, his hair tousled, looking like he'd just gotten up. His face sullen. His eyes red, it looked like, from crying.

"Let me get dressed. I'll go with you," he said firmly, looking more like twelve than nineteen. "I'm not going to resist this."

When the kid came out in jeans and a flannel shirt, Ruiz read him his rights, to which Justin seemed to have no reaction.

Grasso cuffed him.

GRASSO PRESSED RECORD.

Justin Winslow sat across from Ruiz. Grasso took a seat next to the young man. He looked nervous, but his jaw was set. She couldn't tell if it was determination or defiance.

She wasn't fully onboard with the idea that Justin Winslow shot his father in the face that night. Was Justin mad enough to do it? Totally. Was he there during the time his father was shot? Yep, and there was proof. Proof that he was on the premises, within the wi-fi's reach anyway.

Ruiz was stern as he faced down the kid, and it looked to Grasso like a battleship staring down at a dinghy. Justin looked scruffy and out of place, like when her six-year-old nephew Benny had worn an ill-fitting, full three-piece suit as a ringbearer in a family wedding recently.

"Justin, you've been charged with the murder of your father Derrick Winslow."

"I understand what I'm being charged with." He sounded prim, the corners of his mouth turned up in a self-satisfied smile.

"You were there at his house that night. Let me remind

you that you told us you were studying and never left your dorm room that night. You lied to us."

"I went to his house." Justin shifted in his seat, while keeping his eyes focused on Ruiz. "I left right after I went to the bathroom and saw my RA."

"Did you go with the intent to kill your father?"

Justin swallowed hard but maintained eye contact with Ruiz, his lips still curved into a smile.

"Yes, I did."

Grasso turned toward Justin. "Why did you want to kill him?"

Justin seemed thrown off by this. But he soon responded.

"He ruined my life. He wanted nothing to do with me and tried to pretend I didn't exist for twelve years."

"You told us this before," Grasso nodded and looked over at Ruiz. "What made you want to do it *now*?"

"I realized how much I hated him. And how he'd fucked up my life." Justin was talking louder, his face red, as he gave Grasso a self-righteous look. "Detectives, do you know what it's like to have someone wish you didn't exist?"

"Justin, do you remember a family in your old neighborhood on Folsom Road five years ago—the Millers?" Ruiz asked. "They lived close to your old house. Christopher Miller was a few years older than you, I think."

"Christopher tutored me in chess club at middle school. We hung out sometimes," Justin looked down and his finger traced the edge of the handcuff on one hand. I remember that night it happened. I saw the police cars from my window. My mom was freaking out."

"Tell me what details you remember about that night— about what you heard happened to the Millers."

The kid frowned and met Ruiz's eyes. "The family was

shot. And robbed. I heard they took all the computers. And then I found out in the morning—Christopher was dead. I was sad because I knew him."

"You don't remember any more details of the robbery or murders." Ruiz got his stern look back.

"That's all I heard," Justin said. Suddenly he had a look on his face, shame, as if he'd failed a test. "Was there something else that happened?"

"Okay, Justin." Ruiz let out a sigh of frustration and raised an eyebrow at Grasso. He picked up the phone in the room.

Grasso shared his disappointment. Justin was clueless about the methods used in the Miller home invasion. He couldn't have staged a copycat crime.

Ruiz punched a button on the phone and spoke quietly into the receiver. His lips tight, he nodded to the kid.

"Officer Yamashita is going to take you back to the holding cell now."

After Lani Yamashita came in and led the boy away, Ruiz turned off the recording device and closed the door. He paced across the floor along the table.

"Dang it, I wanted to be done with this case, Dani."

Grasso slumped down in her chair. "He was in middle school when the Millers were killed, and he knows what a thirteen-year-old kid would remember—a kid he looked up to was killed. Justin could be lying, but I don't think he has it in him to be good at it."

"Yeah, but the kid was *there*. He wanted to kill his dad. We heard him admit it."

"Justin could have been lurking outside and still logged into the wi-fi. We don't have proof he was inside."

"Yet he's willing to let us think he murdered his dad. He wants to be known as the one who killed him. Like he was proud of it." Ruiz stood up and collected his tablet and paperwork. Suddenly he stopped and looked up. "Maybe that's what he wants. Kind of like he was living through it—-"

"Vicariously?" Grasso offered.

"Exactly. Like he thought the only way his life would be complete and whole was if his father was dead. And wow, he didn't have to do it himself. Someone did it for him. But he's going to claim it. It makes him feel powerful when he's felt powerless for so long."

Grasso thought this was an interesting theory. Ruiz could be on to something. Justin had looked proud, triumphant in the interview, as if he'd scored a personal victory.

"You up for Garcia's?" Ruiz asked. "I got up late and missed breakfast."

"You don't have to twist my arm," Grasso stood up. "Besides, we deserve something after this morning. All that work and no payoff."

It felt good to get up and walk outside. It was a sunny day, with a soft cool breeze blowing, and the nearby wooded hills loomed in the west, fresh and green, looking down on the town. With the sun, more people were out and about. They were headed for Garcia's during the peak lunch hour. If the tables were taken, they'd get theirs to go.

On the way, they ran into Ryan Dawson, wearing sunglasses and carrying a bag from Garcia's. "The whole town's in line today, guys." He grinned. "Good luck."

Charlotte Baldwin, who'd run Rosalind Mabrey's nature foundation, looked both ways and crossed to the other side of the street a few yards in front of them. She was wearing a fancy grey suit and high heels. Ruiz's eyes followed the woman until she made it to the opposite curb, which Grasso thought was interesting.

They walked into the small Mexican café, only to see a line inside at the ordering counter. They immediately joined it. Grasso scanned the dining area. No free tables.

The owner, David Garcia, hailed them with his usual friendly and loud greeting.

"It's Monte Verde's dynamic duo. What can I get you? Jimmy, you always get the same—so we'll get it going. What you want, Dani?"

"Chicken Chili Verde burrito for me, David."

"You got it." David called out in a sing song voice. "Ruiz, we missed you last night in the backroom. Something come up?"

Grasso looked up to see Ruiz's face turning red. He mumbled *shit* under his breath. Ladera's birthday party. With his counseling appointment, Ruiz must have forgotten about it.

"I had a family emergency come up. I was sorry to miss it."

She'd just witnessed a rare event: Ruiz lying. The department should put out some kind of a press release.

They took their food back to Monte Verde's tiny city park. They shoed away some birds and sat down at a picnic table. At the small playground nearby, mothers and fathers were pushing their toddlers on the swing set. Ruiz grabbed his carne asado burrito in his two large hands, unwrapped the top and bit off a hunk. "I forgot Ladera's birthday party. I can't believe I did that."

"Cut yourself some slack. This case has been rough." She sliced her burrito in two with a plastic knife and picked up a half. "Counseling's intense. I know you get anxious about it."

"Ladera didn't deserve that. He was looking at me like a sad puppy this morning, and I walked right past him. I didn't want to deal with him."

"Tell him you're sorry," Grasso said. "It happens. Remember, you were bugging all of us to go to it. You're a lot nicer to him than the rest of us."

Ruiz frowned at her over his burrito. "A low bar, Grasso." She laughed.

Ruiz shook his head and looked up at a bird swooping by on a reconnaissance mission, looking for crumbs.

"I'm going to track down Kira Baker," Grasso took a sip from her water bottle. "I suspect she's the 'Becker' woman Olga mentioned. I didn't account for the accent. Kira Baker was there until 1:30. Maybe she saw something."

"Isn't there an Agatha Christie book, where everyone who has a grudge against the murder victim decides to kill him?" Ruiz took a gulp of his horchata.

"*Murder on the Orient Express*," Grasso said between bites of burrito.

"Maybe that's our answer. With the exception of Olga, everyone had a reason for wanting to kill Derrick Winslow."

AFTER LUNCH, Grasso went to work finding Kira Baker. She found her address—then a resume for her on a tech employment site, which gave her the woman's cell phone number.

"Kira Baker, this is Detective Dani Grasso of the Monte Verde Police Department."

Kira let out a long, heavy sigh. "Yeah. What's up?"

"I believe you were at Derrick Winslow's house in Monte Verde earlier on the day of his murder. Is that true?"

"Yes, I was," the woman said in a choked voice. "During the day. Well—and I was there the night before."

Grasso thought she heard the hiccup of a sob over the phone. "I'd like to ask you some questions. Can I meet you at your address? On California Street in Mountain View?"

"Sure, that's fine. I'm in unit 3."

Grasso parked on the street, which was lined with apartment complexes in nearly every direction she looked. Most of them two or three stories and looking several decades old. Kira's was a nicer looking complex, renovated recently. Lots of white paint brightened things up, and neatly trimmed shrubbery lined the walkways.

She knocked on the door of Kira's apartment, which was on the bottom floor.

"Detective Dani Grasso, Monte Verde Police Department."

Grasso saw a shadow in the peephole. Kira Baker opened the door and invited Grasso in.

Kira Baker was not having a good day. Her eyes were red rimmed, her nose pink and blotchy. Her dark hair hung limply on the shoulders of her bathrobe. She didn't look like the model Olga Kostenko had described. Olga had been right, though. The woman did have big lips. Grasso spent too much time looking at them to try to figure out if they were real.

"Please, come in and have a seat." Kira gestured toward a new-looking leather sofa.

"Thank you, Ms. Baker." Grasso nodded. "Not a great day?"

"I'm still dealing with his loss." Kira dabbed at her eyes with a tissue. "Derrick was very important to me. I can't imagine how this could have happened to him. Who would do this?"

Grasso wanted to say: a lot of people. But she said, calmly, "I'm sorry for your loss, Ms. Baker. I appreciate you letting me ask you some questions. We're doing our best to find his killer."

The woman's lips turned up into a pout.

"I'm glad somebody is, detective."

"You spent the night before the murder at Mr. Winslow's house. Is this something you do often?"

"It had been happening more and more." Kira sniffed and wiped her nose with a tissue. "We met about six months ago. I'd worked as a personal assistant for a business associate of Derrick's, Gordon Howell. He's another venture builder, like Derrick. Gordon had a cocktail party and Derrick came. We started talking and hit it off right away. Later than night, he called me, and we kept talking. A few weeks ago, I broke up with my boyfriend because it was going so well with Derrick."

Grasso looked at Kira and wondered how long it would have been, if Winslow hadn't been killed, before the magic ran out and she saw him for who he was. It had happened for Marcia Winslow Davies.

"When you stayed at Mr. Winslow's house, did you ever notice anyone lurking around outside? Watching the house?"

"I don't think so." Kira put her feet up on a footstool. Her toenails were painted glossy cherry red and adorned with tiny pink hearts. "But Derrick had a lot of people coming in and out. He had the office in downtown Monte Verde, but he was usually having meetings at his house."

With that many people coming and going, it would have been hard to track who was in the house, Grasso thought.

"Did he keep the door locked?"

"Maybe?" Kira said distractedly, as she reached over to

an end table for a tube of hand lotion. "I think the housekeeper let people in when they arrived to meet with Derrick."

"Do you remember him having arguments with anyone at the house? With any of these businesspeople who came to meet with him?"

Kira thought for a moment as she smoothed coconut-scented lotion into her hands. "He argued with his ex-wife. I forget her name—Mary or Marcia, something like that—but she had a son that she kept insisting was Derrick's. I think he's in college. She came to the house that day he was killed, and I got right away that she did *not* like me. *At all.*" Kira held up her hands in kind of a jazz hands way.

"The boy came over sometimes and asked for money for school, and Derrick was always mad afterwards, saying the boy was going to drain him of all his money and he'd have nothing left."

Grasso wanted to tell her that fathers do have a responsibility to pay support for their children. But Kira had already bought into Derrick's narrative. She was grieving his loss, and it wasn't Grasso's job to convince her that her dead boyfriend was a jerk.

"Ms. Baker, do you know where Mr. Winslow kept his gun? Had you seen it before?"

"He had a safe. He told me he kept a gun in there. I never saw him take it out, though." Kira began sobbing again. "And then he was killed with it. Oh, *my God.* His own gun. It was a horrible way to die."

"It *was* a horrible way to die," Grasso agreed. "Do you have any idea who had access to the safe?"

Kira Baker patted her nose with a tissue and shook her head. "Derrick was paranoid about the safe. He yelled at me once for asking about it. But I can understand him being cautious. I don't think anyone in the house had the combination to it."

It looked from her resume that Kira was 29 years old. She made Grasso feel old. She was tired of talking to the woman, who needed a serious lesson in recognizing relationship red flags. She didn't think she'd get anything else out of her, especially since Olga Kostenko said Kira hadn't been there past 1:30 on the day he'd been killed, and she'd only known Derrick Winslow for a short time.

"Ms. Baker, thank you for your time. I'm sorry for your loss. We do want to find who killed Derrick, so if you remember anything else that might be helpful to our investigation, please let me know."

Grasso handed Kira Baker her card and headed for the car.

She hoped there was some pinot grigio left at Tom's, because after today, she needed it.

**16**

———

Ladera was sitting in front of his computer filling out a report when Ruiz came back. Ruiz was tempted to pass him by and get back to work, but he forced himself to stop and talk.

Ruiz often reassured himself that he was a nice guy. A good person. Compliments from his friends, from Grasso and his coworkers reinforced that, and he sometimes felt like he stood a little higher than other people. Lived by a higher set of standards.

Marriage counseling was poking holes in that identity; he didn't get to keep that image of himself anymore. He failed. He snapped at people. He thought about what he was going to say next instead of listening to his wife when she was talking. He judged other people more harshly than he did himself. He thought of himself as performing better at living up to obligations and being a generally nice person—when it wasn't true.

Last night, he'd blown off Ladera's party.

Ruiz stood in front of Ladera's desk.

"Hey, Frank."

Ladera didn't give him his usual grin. Normally the guy was a big, goofy dog. He had a way of loving people unconditionally—while he was annoying them and driving them crazy at the same time. He always came back after a snub with a grin and a shrug.

He wouldn't be doing that today.

Ruiz considered his options and decided to tell the truth. Do that whole vulnerability thing that Jennifer DeGroot LFMT had talked about. Lay it all out honestly. He'd trust that Ladera would understand.

"I want to say I'm sorry for missing your party last night." As people shuffled by them, Ruiz face began to burn, and he lowered his voice. He felt embarrassed to be seen doing this and realized he'd never seen anyone apologize to Ladera. He pulled up a chair next to Ladera's desk. Frank looked up from his screen, but his expression didn't change.

"I meant to be there. I had a counseling session with Reyna. This therapy stuff has been long and painful. But last night we made some progress. Finally. So, we went to dinner together and—we had a great time. I did remember your party, but I chose to stay with Reyna."

Here he was reeling off details of his evening to Frank, whose own marriage counseling experience had been a failure. He was driving in the knife.

"Jimmy. You know, I get it." Frank smiled. "Ryan was there, and Andy Rogers, too. Schallert came. Grasso even stopped by for a few minutes. We had a really good time."

"You did?" Ruiz heard surprise in his own voice.

Ladera nodded. "Yeah. I'm sorry you didn't make it because you're my friend. But I'm happy you and Reyna are working things out. Real happy for you, Jimmy." The look on Ladera's face was genuine.

Ruiz was unable to speak. He had no words to say. There

was no malice in the man's eyes. He slapped Ladera on the back and mumbled something stupid and incomprehensible like, *"hey, well, you're the best, man, good talking to ya. See ya."*

Ruiz went back to one of the interrogation rooms and put his head down on the table, without even thinking of all the grimy hands that had been on it.

Ladera was the better man. No question.

WHEN GRASSO GOT BACK to the station, Ruiz told her he was going to take Justin Winslow back into the interrogation room so they could ask him questions about the night of his father's murder.

"We'll need to let him go. But I need to ask him specifically about the details of the murder and anything he saw." Ruiz swirled the remains of his afternoon coffee in his mug.

"We might want to ask him about his father's gun. If he knew where it was kept." Grasso said tiredly. "Kira Baker told me Winslow kept it in his safe and was really paranoid about anyone getting at it."

"After all of this, he'll have to confess that he didn't really kill his dad." Ruiz said. "That will be interesting."

Within a few minutes, Justin was brought into the interrogation room. He looked angry, as if he was catching on that nobody believed his claim.

He slunk down into the chair, his handcuffed arms stretched out before him. His face looked pale and there were bags under his eyes.

"Why don't you guys leave me alone." He sputtered, casting a fierce look at Ruiz, then Grasso who sat across from him. "You need to book me. Isn't that what you're supposed to do? I shot my father. You know the facts."

"Justin, what's the combo to your father's safe?"

The kid sat stunned to silence, then the corner of his mouth turned up contemptuously. "Why would I know the combo to his safe?"

"*Justin.*" Ruiz sighed in frustration. "There is no proof that you killed your father. Obviously, you wanted to. If you did, where did you get the gun?"

"I found it in a box under his bed," Justin blurted out defiantly.

Ruiz glanced at Grasso, who shrugged. She didn't seem to have any better ideas. He had once had someone call in and confess to murder. An 82-year-old woman who claimed she'd killed her husband. She said it so politely and insistently. It had been easy to figure out that she hadn't done it. Her husband had died of a heart attack two years before.

"Justin, why don't you tell me the story of that night. What made you decide to kill him *that* night? You were in your room studying. You decided to leave and drive over to his house in Monte Verde. What made you decide you wanted to do it?"

The kid came to life, his face flushed with energy. "I couldn't stop thinking about him. What he'd done to me. My mother had an argument with him that day because he still hadn't given me my tuition for winter quarter. It started to get hard to focus on my work. All I could think about was wanting him dead. So, I got dressed and slipped out. Nobody saw me. Most of my dorm floor was at a movie on campus."

Justin's eyes were unnaturally bright, and he looked past

Grasso, as if he were watching the story unfold like a movie on the wall behind her.

"I got there after 10 p.m., I think. I waited in my car. There were lights on in his house, but it was dark outside. Really windy and it had started to rain. I wanted to make sure everyone had left his house before I went in. A van was parked on the street. I didn't know who it was. But around 11, I think, somebody ran out to the van in the rain. Then it screeched and drove away. But I was happy they were gone. It was my chance now."

Thank God Grasso had started the recording, Ruiz thought. They'd have this info to go over. Derrick Winslow was killed sometime before 11. If Justin was telling the truth, whoever had raced away in the car had killed him. Now they just had to figure out who.

Grasso seemed to be taking a conversational approach. She sounded almost casual as she asked her question.

"Any idea if the driver was a man or a woman?"

"I don't think that matters, does it? I was just happy they were gone," Justin said, irritated that she'd asked. "Probably a guy."

"What did you do after the van left?" Ruiz wanted to press him for details, but he could tell just looking at him that the kid was brittle, worn thin by the emotional intensity of the past few days. He was driven to get to the payoff. He wanted to get to the part of the story where he killed his dad.

"I got out of my car and went up to the front door. It was unlocked, which was stupid of the guy who left. Who does that? It's dangerous." He took a deep breath and licked his lips. "I turned the knob and went in. I could hear the business news really loud in my dad's bedroom. He always listened to it, always following the stocks, what was going on in tech. He hated to have somebody know something he didn't. So I went in the room, and I—"

He paused for a long time. He stared blankly at the table. He'd come to a dead end.

"What happened next, Justin?" Ruiz asked, trying to be gentle with the kid. He realized he recognized something in Justin's face. He'd felt it growing up. Ruiz knew what it was like to lay in bed late at night and fantasize that someone who'd hurt you was gone. He remembered imagining it— his own father, Manuel Ruiz, in a crumpled heap on the floor, finally killed by his drinking. Or in the street in front of their apartment complex, run over by a car. Obliterated.

He felt for this kid.

"Where did you shoot him, Justin?" Ruiz felt his throat tighten. He was seeing this with Justin.

"I shot him in the heart." Justin said, unwavering, as he looked at Ruiz. "Right in his chest. He was dead. I could feel it—the gun right there in the palm of my hand. I felt so good, better than I had in my whole life. I *must* have made this happen. Because no one in the world could have hated him as much as I did."

Justin wished for Derrick Winslow to die. And he had. Someone else had pulled the trigger, but as far as Justin was concerned, his hatred had brought about his father's death.

Ruiz shot a glance at Grasso, wondering if she'd come to the same conclusion:

Justin must not have even gone into his father's bedroom. He would have seen the horror of his father's face —and obliterating the face of the man who looked like him would have been too good to leave out of his story. Justin would want to claim that.

Within a half an hour, Marcia Winslow Davies and Kenneth Davies came to the station. They sat next to Justin and held him as he cried. Marcia promised to have him admitted for a psychological examination and treatment for trauma.

Grasso offered to help if she needed someone to go with them, but Mrs. Davies quietly declined.

Marcia and Kenneth sat on either side of Justin, talking in hushed voices about their next steps to help him. Which made Ruiz wonder if Justin had had previous meltdowns like this.

After they left, Ruiz and Grasso sat in chairs across from each other for a while, silent and bleary eyed. Ruiz blotted tears with the sleeve of his jacket, not caring whether Grasso saw him or not.

They weren't sure if any of what they'd just heard from Justin was based in reality. If it was, the van driver was a potential new suspect.

If it wasn't, they were back to square one.

But after what had just happened, they needed a break before they tried to figure out which it was.

THE NEXT MORNING, Grasso awoke from a long, much-needed sleep.

She turned over in the bed to see Tom, supported on his elbow, looking down at her.

"Hey, what are you doing?"

She brushed her hair from her eyes.

He grinned at her, like a kid preparing to see a new Star Wars movie for the first time.

"We're having dinner at Unnon's tonight," he said. "I can't wait."

*Shit.* She sat up and blinked—with the intensity of the

Winslow case, Grasso's days had blurred into her nights. She didn't have a good sense of what day of the week it was. But she fumbled for her phone on the nightstand and checked her calendar. Sure, enough, the dinner was tonight.

"I'm glad *you're* excited." She sat up and bopped him with her pillow.

"You know, I really am." He studied her face for a while and gave her an odd look. "I'm a little sad that you're seeing this as an ordeal to go through."

Then he pulled the pillow from under his arm and bopped her back. He bent down over her and gave her a long slow kiss. Which ended any resistance on her part. Soon things escalated and it was clear they wouldn't be getting out of bed anytime soon.

After her shower, she pulled on a robe and went downstairs to make coffee and check messages.

Marcia Davies texted her thanks for their help with Justin and said he would be in a facility for a few days where he could get some rest and 24-hour attention and care.

Then she saw Anthony's text:

> THE ENTIRE FAMILY KNOWS ABOUT TOM.
> MY JOB IS DONE.

It took everything in her for Grasso to not text back an expletive.

It would be a full day, and then they'd head for Saratoga to Unnon's. It gave her some comfort that Tom didn't seem worried at all about meeting Giovanni Grasso.

But she'd lived 25 years embedded in the Grasso family structure.

She could smile at Tom's carefree anticipation, knowing that he did not know these people like she did.

Oh, he had no idea.

**17**

———

"Let's look at possible suspects." Ruiz sat down across from Grasso that morning in a briefing room. "People we might need to talk to again." Grasso got up and started a list on the white board.

"Things were bad between Michael Fisk and Winslow. He was working out in his home gym that night." Grasso said. "Though it would be easy for him to tamper with the time stamps and head up to Monte Verde. But I think he's off the list, since Conor Doyle said he called him at 10:35 p.m."

Ruiz nodded reluctantly. "What about Jeff Gabbard?"

"Jeff Gabbard's personal assistant confirmed he was having a late dinner with coworkers up in San Francisco." Grasso hesitated with the marker in her hand. "They left to come back at 10:15. Looks like that *might* get him off the hook, since it's a 45-minute drive down to Monte Verde."

"Put him on the list. It's still possible." Ruiz said, dumping a sugar-free sweetener into his coffee mug.

Grasso began writing. "Marcia Winslow Davies. She was supposedly home that night, but again, she had a motive, same as Justin. She only has Kenneth Davies to vouch for her. And she was just a few miles away."

"She's a possibility. She was angry on Justin's behalf." Ruiz sat back and ate a spoonful of nonfat, sugar-free yogurt, turning the spoon over on his tongue. Probably trying to suck some flavor out of the weak stuff, Grasso thought.

"What about Justin's story about the person who ran out of Winslow's house that night?" Grasso asked. "He was parked on the street, according to Justin."

"You trust Justin's story, Grasso? When he was hallucinating for most of the interrogation?"

"I remember Justin getting mad when I asked about the driver," Grasso said. "He said 'that doesn't really matter, does it?' He saw something and I believe it. The only thing off in his story was that he didn't actually kill his dad."

Ruiz looked skeptical. "If he'd actually seen someone, and if it did turn out to be a person who could have killed Winslow—it would be unreliable testimony, because of his mental state."

"Wait a minute. I just thought of this," she said, blinking. "She mentioned it, but I didn't think much of it at the time. Kira Baker told me she broke up with her boyfriend after she started dating Derrick."

"Okay. Find out who he is and let's talk to him." Ruiz said. "If he was killing out of jealousy, he went to a lot of trouble to do it. Crimes of passion aren't usually that well thought out."

"I'll talk to her after ten." Grasso smirked. "Like Olga Kostenko said, she's a very late sleeper."

Ruiz finished his yogurt, wiped off his spoon and tossed the container in the garbage can.

"We could be back where we started. This could be what

it looked like at first—a home invasion robbery and murder. Maybe it was related to the Millers."

He got up and used his phone to take a photo of the list she'd written on the board. He liked to keep these things with him, Grasso knew, whenever he thought about a case, which was pretty much day and night.

"I'm going to drive up to Winslow's house, to see where the van might have parked." Ruiz said. "Let me know what you hear from Kira Baker."

Grasso did have other work to do—a report that she'd been putting off, and a couple of phone calls to return about a previous case. So, she settled in at the computer to crank out the work, while waiting for Kira Baker to wake up. And thinking about tonight's dinner with her grandfather.

Tom was so lighthearted about the get-together, it made Grasso nervous. Nice that he wasn't worrying, but what if he said something stupid? What if he broke one of the many unwritten Grasso rules—since he didn't know them? She wondered if she could handle it if Unnon ended up disliking Tom. If he thought Tom was too old or rejected him for any other reason, she'd have to again hold her ground. And risk being shunned by the family, like she had when she'd taken the MVPD job.

After she'd returned the calls and submitted one of the reports, Grasso called Kira Baker.

Kira sounded like she'd just woken up. It took her a while to realize who it was who was calling. "Oh, that's right. Detective Grasso. I remember. What was it that you wanted to ask?"

"You mentioned that you were dating someone before you met Derrick. How angry was this boyfriend when you broke up with him?"

Kira sighed. "He was really pissed off at me. He said I

tricked him into believing I cared for him. That we had something really special."

It sounded like this guy was as bad as Kira at not noticing red flags.

"How long were you with him?" Grasso was distracted by Ruiz trying to get her attention from his computer across the room.

"It was about—maybe eight months." Kira trailed off. "I really liked him and all, but he went on and on about how I'd deceived him. He didn't understand what happened. He followed me one day when I was going to meet Derrick for lunch. It creeped me out."

"Kira, please give me his name." Grasso said firmly.

"His name is Mario. He's a cop, too. In San Jose."

GRASSO HUNG UP.

She entered her notes right after the call, so she didn't forget the details of what Kira had said.

Mario Flores.

Ruiz hadn't told her much about him, but she remembered his name. He was a cop.

Ruiz connected with her eyes. She shot him the *holy-crap-get-over-here* look.

Ruiz came over to her desk. He had a strange, glazed look in his eyes.

"Kira's boyfriend. Was his name Mario Flores?"

"Yeah." She tried to figure out how Ruiz could have known this. "Is it the same person who—"

One look at Ruiz's face and Grasso couldn't finish the sentence. "He's a cop. SJPD Homicide."

Ruiz shifted on his feet. "Crime Scene finally identified

the prints on the wall of Derrick's house. They're his." A vein pulsed in his forehead.

"Kira said Mario got angry when she broke up with him."

"Call Flores. Get him in for questioning—today. You can handle this. I won't be there."

With that, Ruiz went back to his desk, bent his head down and seemed to be hard at work.

She understood why it needed to be her job. She wondered if Ruiz would step away from the case entirely because of conflict of interest.

She called San Jose Homicide and asked for Detective Mario Flores. In a minute or two, a voice came on the line.

"Detective Mario Flores."

"Detective Dani Grasso of Monte Verde Police Department. We need you to come in to answer some questions for us about the murder of Derrick Winslow."

There was a long pause before she heard Flores's voice. It sounded strained and quiet, like he was keeping it low so people in his office didn't hear.

"I can come in during the lunch hour. 12:30." Flores kept it short.

Ruiz didn't talk to her all morning. Grasso finished off another report and a Miracle Whip chicken salad sandwich from Tom. This time Tom had put finely chopped celery and some spice in it that seemed to cut the sweetness. She was surprised to say it, but it was a damn good sandwich.

Grasso prepared for her meeting with Mario Flores, compiling a list of questions on the tablet. She wanted to pull someone else in, like Rogers, since he'd been there that night of the murder, but he wasn't due in for another five hours. Ladera was available, and he was a detective. She couldn't dismiss the idea. But she'd never worked a case with the guy, so she didn't know him or his methods.

She could have done this herself, but she wanted another person there—both for their perspective on the suspect and for the back and forth of two people questioning.

Ladera was sitting at his desk a few feet away shuffling through papers.

"Hey, Frank," she called to him. He looked up. "Can you come here for a minute?"

Dutifully, the man got up eagerly and headed for her desk. "What's up Grasso?"

She motioned for him to have a seat.

"I'm interviewing a possible suspect. He's coming in at 12:30. Ruiz knows this person and is recusing himself for the interview. Can you sit in with me?" She gave him a brief summary of the case as it stood so far, leaving out details of Ruiz's personal connection.

"Sure thing, Grasso. I'll give it a try." Ladera looked thrilled to have been asked. "It's a lot more interesting than the shoplifting report I'm working on."

RUIZ GOT UP, grabbed his coat, and walked out the back.

He didn't know where he was going, but he needed to get out. There was a chemical pumping through his veins, buzzing through his arms, his legs, his brain.

He walked away from downtown. He didn't want to see anyone he knew. Didn't want to talk to anyone and have to be cheerful. He went down an alley that led to a hilly, suburban street, a row of colorful California bungalows, small stucco houses with curved arches over front porches and tiny windows. Two and a half-million-dollar properties, though they had as much space as one-bedroom apartments.

His feet were moving now without him having to think about where they were going.

He hadn't wanted to hear the name again. It was hard enough hearing it in the counseling room. The reason he was even doing marriage counseling was because of what Flores had done. Flores had opened up a rift in his home, and now he and Reyna spent every Thursday night trying to patch it up. A string of swear words let loose in his brain and he wanted to shout them at the fuzzy little rat dogs being walked by their owners and the stylish couples heading for their fancy fucking cafes on Main Street.

The anger burned like a fire in his gut. He saw Flores's face, his perfect jawline, and those brown eyes that women seemed unable to resist. Flores had taken something from him that he'd never get back.

He'd found out about Flores and Reyna last year from the redheaded woman, Mandy, from the SJPD. The day he and Flores solved the Schuler case, she'd called and told Ruiz what she'd seen.

He'd met with Flores to tell him to never see, contact, or talk to his wife again. He'd gone into crisis mode, trying to control the situation. He hadn't allowed himself to be angry —he didn't want to be distracted. But the anger had grown in him, from a small seed he'd noticed when he met with Flores that last time, to a spiny growth that spread out into his body and began to choke off not Flores's life, but his own.

A small red light flicked on in Ruiz's brain. This was the time.

Now everything Flores had would be taken from him.

The information they had on him, the fingerprints on Winslow's wall, the stalking of the ex-girlfriend. Ruiz remembered that Flores had done this before. Some girl named Oksana, whom he'd followed for a while after she'd broken up with him. Flores was so full of himself, he couldn't believe she'd actually left him.

Ruiz could not do this himself. He wouldn't even need to. Flores had brought this on himself.

Ruiz would sit back and watch this play out.

The fall of Mario Flores would happen on Ruiz's own turf.

**18**

———

At 12:35, Grasso got a call from reception that Detective Flores was here. She met him at the door and buzzed him in. She motioned to Ladera that this was it. She'd spent a half hour filling the detective in on the case.

Ruiz was not at his desk.

Flores was dressed in a navy suit and a blue and gold tie a little too fancy for a detective. The SJPD logo pin on his tie was one of the most badass department logos she'd seen, a red ring that read SJ HOMICIDE, surrounding a black swan ready to fly into the air.

Flores was about three inches taller than she was and had warm brown eyes and a very expensive haircut. He obviously put in hours at the gym and had a "look." It didn't do much for her, but she could see how Reyna Ruiz would go for this guy.

"Detective, thank you for coming in."

She led him to the interrogation room. Flores looked around as they walked and seemed fascinated by this glimpse into the workings of a much smaller police operation.

"Detective Ladera will be joining us. Please have a seat, Detective Flores."

Flores took a seat across from her, as Ladera entered with a notebook and sat down next to Grasso. Grasso got up to push the button to record the session.

"I'll get to the point, Detective. Crime scene found your fingerprints in Derrick Winslow's house."

Flores suddenly looked pale. He lowered his head, and she could hear him take in a breath.

"Did you know Derrick Winslow?"

Flores swallowed. "I met him. I didn't know him well."

"But you do know Kira Baker."

Flores blinked and looked down at the table. "We went out for a while. Several months."

"Last month she broke off your relationship. Is that true?'

"She told me she had started seeing Derrick Winslow and wanted to end our relationship."

"That must have hurt," Grasso said sympathetically. The man looked genuinely heartbroken. "How did you react to that?"

"Like anybody would. It was painful to hear. I thought everything was good, that we were good. The news upset me."

"Were you angry?"

"Of course I was. She wasn't honest with me."

"Did you follow Kira Baker – stalk her?"

"I followed her one night because I wanted to find out who she was seeing."

"You know that doesn't look good for you." Grasso watched this guy, who supposedly wooed women right and left. Was he that clueless? "Women don't like when you do that."

Flores sighed and lifted a hand in frustration. "Suddenly the relationship was over. I wanted to see who she left me for."

"How did you feel about Mr. Winslow?"

"Not great. He took my girlfriend away from me." He met Grasso's eyes. "But I didn't want to kill him." At least someone could say that.

Now Ladera put his arms on the table and leaned forward, an intense look in his eyes. "So tell me. What time did you go to Winslow's house?"

Flores sat for a while. He rubbed his eyes, then his lip twitched.

"I got there at about 9:30. I went in and confronted Winslow. He said some pretty nasty things to me. It didn't go well, and I left by 10 p.m."

The medical report estimated Winslow's time of death as somewhere between 10 and 11 p.m. With the give-or-take nature of the estimate, it was quite possible Flores could have done it.

"Can anyone vouch for your return?"

Flores shrugged. "Someplace Bar and Grill. I went there immediately afterwards. I was there till about 11:30. The owner and his daughter talked to me—and a lot of other people. It's a cop hangout."

*Duh, Captain Obvious.* Everyone Grasso worked with had been there at some point.

"When you were at Winslow's, did you see anyone else around the house?"

Flores tightened his lips. "I saw someone in a Honda Civic parked on the street, between Winslow's house and the next. I thought that was weird, considering it's a pretty remote area. It was some young guy."

Justin was in his car when Flores was there. The timetable was being filled in, even if Grasso wasn't sure she was getting very far with Flores. She believed he could get angry enough to kill Winslow. He would have known the details of the Miller home invasion and murders. He'd have access to the database, so he could have set up the scene at Winslow's to match the Millers'.

"So you told him who you were," Grasso said. "How did that go?"

Flores rubbed his eyes. It was a minute or two before he spoke.

"Winslow looked tired and wasn't happy to see me once I told him who I was. I said I wanted to talk, and we went inside."

"What condition was the house in when you were there?"

"It hadn't been ransacked, if that's what you're asking." Flores tried to read her face.

Ladera had been following along, and he was getting into this. He leaned his elbows on the table and asked, in a gruff voice:

"Tell us what parts of the house he took you through."

Flores closed his eyes, as if trying to visualize it. "We went through the dining area and then up the stairs. We sat down in his office and talked. For about thirty minutes. Then I walked out, same way I came in, and I left."

The prints had been on the stairwell near the office. His story made sense.

"Tell me about the office, Flores." Grasso wanted to know about the safe. "Tell me exactly what you saw in the room."

"He had two computers set up on his desk. Several filing cabinets. Awards on the walls. Lots of photos of himself, framed." Flores said, with a look of distaste on his face. "A bookshelf. In the corner was a black metal safe, about three feet high. Looked like it had a keycode mechanism, like mine."

"Was the safe open? Closed?"

"Closed."

"Mario," Grasso looked at the man, who looked pale, stressed and sleep deprived. "You're a detective. From what you could tell—did it seem like anyone else was in the house?"

"I really can't say. It's a big house. There could have been someone upstairs." He grimaced and rubbed his forehead. "I guess my spidey sense wasn't working that day," he said sarcastically.

"When you talked with Winslow, you said he 'said some nasty things,'" Grasso pointed out. "What did he say?"

Flores's eye twitched. "He used a racial slur that I don't want to repeat. And he implied that I could not, *uh*—make Kira happy like he could."

Grasso had grown up with two older brothers. She knew what a pissing contest was. Winslow had tried to provoke Flores.

"And how did you respond?"

"I turned it back on him and said someone like me could satisfy Kira in ways an older man could only dream of."

As someone dating an older man, Grasso found this humorous—and not true to her experience. It was a nice comeback though.

"What happened then?" Grasso was genuinely curious. "What did he say?"

"He punched me in the face," Flores responded. He

turned his head toward her and pointed at a greyish bruise on his cheekbone.

"You let that slide? Or did you fight back?" Grasso leaned back in her chair and watched him.

"I love my job, and I had no intention of losing it over this." Flores said, his face serious, believable—maybe even pleading with her. "I got up and walked out."

That seemed way too easy. When Flores got talking, he was smooth. A smart, persuasive guy. But he was also a man of pride. He could plead a case well and convince people he had done the only reasonable thing, given his circumstances. Yet he couldn't resist the lure of winning a fight. At that stage of the game, given his sassy comeback to Winslow, she couldn't imagine that Flores would have let it go.

"You walked out. After a man who'd stolen your girlfriend had insulted you, then *hit* you." Flores was probably already upset. This must have been gasoline on the fire. "Tell me, Flores, how you did this. Because I'm having a hard time believing you walked away after he hit you."

Flores looked dazed for a moment. He sat back in his chair, his arms tightly at his sides. Sweat made his forehead shine.

"My job is all I have left. I've fucked up many times. Every time it's cost me."

Flores's watery brown eyes now made him look vulnerable and weak. Someone lacking the courage to kill. Was this a ploy? If so, he was *good*.

"Derrick Winslow was a narcissistic, cruel person. If anyone should have died, it was him," Flores said hoarsely. "But I made up my mind that night. I would not be the one to do it."

Grasso caught Ladera's eye and nodded. She needed to leave the room for a few minutes, to make sure she was being clearheaded in her judgment.

"Excuse me." She flashed Flores a stern look then got up and left the room, in a move she'd seen Ruiz do once. Keep the suspect on edge, confused. Let him simmer for a few minutes, then go back in the room and see if he had something else to say.

After the interview, she could confirm Flores had been at Winslow's the night of the murder. He'd been angry at the man. But she didn't believe he'd set up the home invasion.

She also didn't believe he'd walk away from his showdown with Winslow. She wondered if there was something he was leaving out.

If Flores fled town, he'd lose the job he seemed to genuinely love. His only way out was to hang in there, answer all the questions he was asked and see this case through.

After a trip to the ladies room and a refill on her coffee, Grasso went back into the interrogation room and told Mario Flores he could go.

She texted Ruiz, whom she suspected had left the station while Flores was there for the interview.

I let him go. His answers made sense. He's not a flight risk.

Yeah. He doesn't want to lose his job.

She heard nothing back.

A half hour later, she looked up to see Ruiz at his desk. She shot a look at him and texted.

Wanna talk?

He met her in the interrogation room. He scowled—his angry bear look, which she was quite familiar with. It didn't faze her anymore.

"You let him walk out of here."

"I couldn't keep him." Grasso said. "Everything he said made sense. I pulled Ladera in for the questioning, and he thought so, too. The timing, the fingerprints. I just called Someplace Bar and Grill. Mr. Kelly, the owner, verified that they saw him come in a little before 10:15 p.m. Flores was probably mad enough to kill Winslow. I don't think he did, but I'm not sure he didn't leave some details out."

Ruiz slunk down into the office chair. "He'd know about the Miller case and have access to info on it. Flores was there that night at Winslow's. He had a motive. You shouldn't have let him go, Dani."

Grasso hadn't seen this look on his face before. Ruiz was disappointed in her, and it hurt like hell. As much as anything her parents could ever say to her.

But her conscience wouldn't let her make any other decision.

She couldn't believe the words that came out of her mouth next.

"You recused yourself, Jimmy." Tears were stinging her eyes. "I am doing the job you trained me to do. If you're making judgements based on what's happened in your personal life, you shouldn't be on the case."

Ruiz listened to her, expressionless. He pushed his chair back, got up and left the room.

When he left Monte Verde, Flores wanted badly to head to Someplace Bar and Grill for a mid-day glass of bourbon.

To feel that soothing warmth wash over him, some solace while he faced the continuing list of mistakes he'd made in the past week.

Instead, he stayed on Highway 280, crossing the valley until he got on 87 to head back to SJ Homicide. Fear vibrated inside him, making his hands shaky on the wheel. He was fighting for his job. A year and a half ago, he'd risen to a position of respect and leadership, and he had taken that privilege for granted. Now he was fighting to get back to where he'd been.

If things went south with the Winslow case, he'd lose his job for good. And one of the detectives on that case happened to be the husband of the woman he'd had an affair with. He already had a big strike against him.

He wanted to talk to his sister, Dawn. For reassurance from someone who knew all his stuff and still loved him. Dawn was sarcastic and made fun of him, but she told him the truth.

He'd become good at making up these conversations in his head, something he liked to call *The Dawn App*. It wasn't as painful as hearing Dawn's actual voice since he could control her reactions.

*So, Dawn, here's something fun: Detectives just questioned me about the Winslow murder. You know, the guy who stole my girlfriend? I went over to talk to Winslow, to ask him what happened with Kira. Lucky me, I was there the night he was murdered.*

*Jesus, Mario, how do you get these women? I am shaking my head right now, if you can't see. I know you well enough to say you probably didn't kill the guy. I say* probably. *If you didn't, you should be fine, right? After this, maybe take a break from women. Stay away from the married ones. The crazy ones. The ones who are still taking resumes.*

He turned onto Guadalupe Parkway to head into the final approach to the station. Two days until his meeting with Buckley to try to move back to leading a team. It had been a year since his fall from grace. Staying where he was —resisting the desire to move anywhere else in the country —had taken every bit of his strength. Really, what was the point? Wherever he went, he'd be taking himself along.

Hadn't he worked to prove he was worthy? Hadn't he been patient with Jesperson's plodding leadership?

Hadn't he told Reyna Ruiz that she needed to either get marriage counseling or leave Jimmy? He'd told her in no uncertain terms—that he didn't want her, and she needed to make a decision out of fairness to Jimmy.

He'd made some mistakes. But he'd also done good things, hadn't he? Now those would go to waste.

Those gold stars in a row next to his name in the past year. If he was arrested for Derrick Winslow's murder, they all went away.

RUIZ SAT AT THE DESK, going through the motions of completing a report he'd promised Schallert he'd turn in.

He'd taken a break from the Winslow case for the rest of his day. Grasso had stepped up to take care of the interviews today. He knew it was the right thing to do.

Grasso didn't do what Ruiz would have done. He couldn't see why she hadn't arrested Flores. She insisted she couldn't have done anything else.

He watched her across the room, at her desk, her eyes fixed on her computer screen. She looked unhappy. When he'd told her she'd made the wrong decision, she looked devastated. But true to what he knew about Grasso, she held her ground and told him maybe he shouldn't even be on the case.

Ruiz had felt this before, and he'd talked to other detectives about it. The times when you *want* a particular suspect to be innocent—or guilty. It shaped what you saw and what you overlooked.

Once they'd realized Flores's connection, something inside him made him not want to pursue other leads. He was done.

He wanted things to slide into place, through his inaction, so that Detective Mario Flores was arrested. An arrest, even the suspicion that he had murdered Winslow, would be enough to tank Flores's career.

The feeling slid through Ruiz like an icy cold steel blade, and he shivered. The desire for revenge felt deliciously good. He was not used to feeling this way. Not since he was a child and, like Justin Winslow, he'd hoped that his abusive father would die in his sleep.

It gave him a sense of sureness—if Flores was arrested, he knew he could move on with his life. He would be happy then, he told himself.

Justice would be done. He'd finally be free.

## 19

Grasso left at 4:30 p.m., since she and Tom needed to be at her grandfather's place for dinner at 6 p.m.

She pulled into the garage and got out of the Mini Cooper, feeling *so* not up to this dinner. After her day, and her disagreement with Ruiz, she didn't feel like experiencing any family drama. She didn't want to go tonight.

When she came into the kitchen, Tom was dressed in a nice casual suit, and a cornflower blue shirt that made his eyes glow in all their exotic, midwestern blueness. He was sitting at the marble island, tapping away on his laptop.

"You look great." She looked him over and said it almost begrudgingly.

He still looked excited about going, a sense of adventure in his eyes. For him this was a challenge, like a brand-new role playing game (RPG) that all the reviewers warned was tough.

Tom sobered up when he saw her face. "How was your day?"

"Any Pinot Grigio left?" She went over to a stash of wine bottles on the counter.

"Dani. Want to talk about it?" He closed his laptop and turned around to face her.

She did *not* want to talk about it. If she said what she was feeling, she couldn't leave it in the back of her mind anymore.

Tom had such an earnest look on his face, she finally spoke up.

"Ruiz and I had a disagreement." She found an interesting bottle of pinot noir and pulled a wine glass down from the rack to pour some. She'd allow herself half a glass. "I made a decision to let a person of interest go, and Ruiz basically told me he's disappointed in me. Angry even."

"Sometimes people you work with disagree with you." Tom said. "I can't imagine you making a decision without considering all the factors, Dani."

She took a sip of the wine. As soon as she tasted it, she knew it wasn't what she was looking for.

"I did the right thing." She said firmly. She gained some confidence from hearing herself say it. "But Ruiz is my mentor. I feel like I'm in uncharted territory disagreeing with him. I've always trusted him, his motives, his experience. I feel he's off base here. It just feels...weird. Wrong."

She took a seat across the marble island from him. He reached his hand out to hers.

"And you're stressed about tonight."

She widened her eyes at him. *Gee, you think?*

"Let's cancel." Tom said softly.

Grasso shook her head. No matter how tempting the idea was. "You don't know how big a deal this is, even for the members of my family who *aren't* going."

"Fine." He sighed, then sat back and looked at her. She wondered what he was thinking. He seemed puzzled, annoyed even.

"Well, if we're going to head right into the storm, you need to go get yourself ready."

Grasso went upstairs to the bedroom and went through her closet and dresser looking for ideas as to what to wear. She'd avoided thinking about this all week.

She decided on a little black dress, her version of the suit Tom wore to upper management meeting at Infinitas. A uniform, always appropriate, but with a neckline low enough to make her feel like a real grown-up lady. She didn't have to second guess her choice, and she liked that. She slipped it on and smoothed it over her hips. She reached into the top drawer of her dresser and took out a necklace that Tom had gotten her on his trip to Vegas last fall—a simple diamond on a light, almost weightless gold chain that slithered through her fingers. She almost dropped it, then managed to catch it and hook the two ends at the back of her neck herself, feeling the cool metal against her neck.

She stepped back to look at herself in the full-length mirror. She barely recognized herself, but she liked the person looking back. Someone who spoke her mind. Who made her own choices. She had grown up with the assumption that there were no choices left for her to make; she simply had to follow the footprints painted on the ground before her.

*Look how easy it is, Dani, just make your way down the path we've prepared for you. We've worked it all out. Don't bother thinking about it. Our way is safer. Better for the family.*

She looked at her face, her lips bright with lipstick, which she'd avoided since some ridiculous experiments with it in high school. Who was this person? She had changed in the past year. She'd turned down a job in the family business. She swore worse than her brothers now—was it just hanging out with cops? She'd disagreed with her family and now her boss.

She slid her feet into a pair of high heels. The only ones she owned, purchased for her graduation from San Jose State, and made her way down the stairs.

Tom stared at her open-mouthed when she entered the kitchen.

"Holy shit," he said, grinning. "Let's go take on the boss."

UNNON LOVED OUTDOOR DINING, even when the weather was 40 degrees—cold to all other Californians. He seemed unaffected by it, even as she shivered in her light dress with a jacket.

As always, his enormous patio dining area was magical—draped with strings of Edison bulbs that cast a warm, soft light on the patio's stone mosaic. At the edge of the lawn, a modernist, life-sized statue of St. Francis of Assisi looked down on them, as if he were their host for the evening. When she was six, Alex and Anthony had told her it was a robot that came to life at night to do Unnon's bidding. She'd been terrified of it.

When Giovanni Grasso led her and Tom to the back patio to a table laden with meat, cheeses, and bread, she saw him limp, something she hadn't seen before. Unnon's stroke last year must have affected him more than she thought.

Milvia, Unnon's chef, came out in her white chef's coat and hugged Dani and Tom, then explained the different foods on the table and what was to come in the remaining courses.

"I should have skipped lunch today." Tom laughed. "I don't know how I'm going to eat all this, but I'm going to try."

"What you can't eat, you take home." Milvia waved at him dismissively. "Dani lived off these leftovers in college. Didn't she tell you?"

"My roommates did, too. They were very happy to see me when I came back from the weekend." Dani smiled.

"Let's put the heaters on for you two." Milvia walked away and turned on the two outdoor heaters on the patio. Suddenly the cold evening became warm and inviting. It made Dani start to loosen up, though she resisted it.

Unnon came out with a bottle of wine and poured glasses for them. Dani immediately began downing her wine.

"What kind of wine is this, Mr. Grasso?" Tom held the wine up to the string of lights above them to look through it. "I love red wine."

"This—" Unnon raised his full glass, "is a wine from where I grew up, in the south of Italy. *Aglianico.* It is *robusto,* like the black grapes it's made from. Hardy and strong— these grapes are our hope when the climate turns hotter because they will survive."

Tom took a sip from his glass and opened his eyes wide, as if he'd just bitten into a ghost pepper.

"Oh boy." He gulped, then coughed. "Now that's a wine that wrestles you to the ground."

Dani handed Tom a plate and began loading up her own from the table, with prosciutto, rustic bread, peppers, caprese salad with fat slices of *mozzarella di bufalo,* fresh basil and tomatoes, and bowls of Italian olives, including the green, buttery *cerignola* olives she loved.

"When you're ready, let's sit down." Unnon waved them toward the large, round wrought-iron table. "I am glad that you're here, Tom. It sounds like you are important to my granddaughter. I want to get to know you."

At this, Dani's chest tightened. Her cheeks burned. Soon it would start. The questioning, the judging looks. The vetting. Her grandfather would certainly grill Tom. He'd ask about his job. Then about his family. Maybe inquire, directly or indirectly, how serious Tom was about his granddaughter.

She poured herself more *aglianico* and brought her plate to the table, where Tom took the chair next to her.

Giovanni Grasso hobbled to a chair across the table from them and eased himself into his seat. He raised his wine glass and the three of them clinked their glasses together.

"I had not been in the country very long before I met Elena. The friends I worked with at the produce market set me up with her. She was very shy, and I don't think we talked very much on our first date. I didn't have much money, so we went for a walk, and I bought her an ice cream. I'd been saving up for that. That went a long way because she loved ice cream."

Dani barely remembered her grandmother, who'd died when she was five. She had white hair and a strong accent and used to get down on the carpet and build things out of blocks with her.

"What was she like, Mr. Grasso?" Tom asked after he finished a bit of caprese salad.

"She was from the north, near Florence. She played piano. Beautifully." Unnon's eyes had a faraway look. "After I took her home, I walked back to my apartment. In the alley, I could hear her start to practice. It echoed in the night. Beautiful notes falling on me like rain."

Dani reached over to replenish the pile of *cerignolas* on her plate. It struck her that her grandfather would not be telling them these personal details if he didn't like Tom, if he was suspicious or had a problem with him. That made her relax a little.

"I think I remember her playing when I was little." Dani said, as a mental picture came to her. "She had played something on the baby grand in your living room. When she finished, I climbed onto the piano bench and started pounding on the keys. I thought, well, if she just did it. I can do it."

Unnon laughed. "That sounds very much like something you would do, Daniela."

Tom leaned forward, curious. "Any other things she did as a child?"

Unnon wiped his face with a napkin, dabbing at his very black mustache.

"Let me see. There was the time my mother had come over from Italy for a visit. She did not speak English. She and Daniela got along very well." He turned to her. "I think you were four or five. Do you remember how you spoke *Italian* to her?"

When the memory came back to her—or rather the memory of family telling her about it, she smiled. As a child she'd sat next to the old lady and reeled off a series of nonsense syllables, while the woman nodded and smiled as if she were understanding everything. Her brothers, five and six years older than her back then, had laughed and teased her about it for years.

"I spoke a lot of nonsense words," Dani said sheepishly.

"I moved my hands around a lot. I thought I was speaking Italian."

Unnon turned to Tom, who had been trying to repress a laugh, and poured more wine into his glass.

"Now Tom, where are you from? Everybody in this valley seems to come from someplace else."

Tom's blue eyes brightened. "I'm from Iowa. A small town outside Des Moines. It's just my mother and my sister back there now—my father died while I was in high school. I moved out here to go to Stanford and fell in love with this place. I started a company with my friends after I graduated." He looked up as he thought for a moment. "That was—oh, God, twenty-four years ago now."

Giovanni Grasso frowned. "So, a lot older than Daniela. You are what—forty-six?"

Tom nodded, the faint smile never leaving his face. He did not seem rattled. He dipped a slice of lacy ciabatta into the seasoned olive oil. The table was silent. When he crunched into the slice, it seemed unnaturally loud.

Unnon sipped his wine. It took forever for him to say something.

"When you get older, you realize what is important," Unnon shrugged, taking a sip of *aglianico*. "That is not a bad thing."

"I've seen how easy it is to give your life away to a job and forget everything else." Tom said, thoughtfully, after he'd finished the ciabatta. "I've learned some hard lessons. My wife divorced me years ago because I was married to my work. Between her job and mine, I never saw her. I knew what I was doing, but I couldn't stop myself. You get on the treadmill, so focused."

Dani watched Tom, who looked as if he were talking to

an old friend, leaning across the table in Unnon's direction. He was being himself, just as he would be with her. He didn't seem afraid of Giovanni Grasso, and the two seemed to be bonding. She should be happy. But the conversation was now between her grandfather and Tom, and she started to feel uncomfortable. As if she weren't there.

"You work in operations, Tom?" Unnon asked, and Tom went on to describe his job to him, in detail. Bored, Dani's thoughts turned back to the Winslow case for a few minutes, trying to figure out how to talk to Ruiz about it tomorrow—something she needed to do.

Unnon nodded, asking questions as Tom talked. Dani soon lost all track of their conversation and got up to go into the kitchen to see if Milvia had something lighter than the *aglianico* to drink.

Milvia had three different burners going on the gas stove, and was deftly moving between the three, tossing and stirring.

"Dani, what can I get you?" Milvia asked, as she looked up for a second. "More wine? You look stunning, by the way."

"Got some *sangiovese*? I need something lighter."

"Over there on the counter." Milvia jerked her head in that direction. "How's it going out there?"

"The two of them have entered their own world." Dani said wryly, as she searched the counter for a corkscrew. "They're talking business."

She found a corkscrew in the drawer, slashed at the foil with its end and peeled it off the top of the bottle. She proceeded to wind it into the cork.

"Looks like your grandfather is getting along well with Tom," Milvia said, as she took a pot of pasta over to the sink.

She dumped spaghetti noodles into a colander. "Were you worried?"

Dani looked up as she pressed in on the levers of the corkscrew to pull out the cork.

"Tom's older. He's not Italian. Unnon can be a tough judge." She pulled out the cork with a loud *thwop*. "I prepared myself tonight. That he'd be rejected. And I decided it didn't matter to me."

The steam rose up from the hot pasta, which Milvia put back in its pan.

"But what if he thinks Tom's great? What are you going to do then? Have you thought about that?"

Dani found herself annoyed by the questions. "I don't get what you're asking."

Milvia poured sauce over the spaghetti, and Dani smelled the sharp tang of fresh clams and garlic. This would be *primi piatti*, the first course after the appetizers. A roast lamb with balsamic vinegar and sage, *secondi piatti*, was pumping out rich smells from the oven. As Milvia tossed the spaghetti in the sauce, she looked up at Dani.

"You're the only kid in the family who talks back to your grandfather. Alex and Anthony don't. Your cousins don't. He's crazy about you—you must know that. You two have had quite a few fights over the years. Maybe you've gotten a little too used to it."

Dani raised her eyebrows. "How could I not get used to it? He wants me to do what *he* thinks is best. Then when he finally told me he was okay with me not working at the store, he wouldn't tell the rest of the family. Everybody still hated me."

"For the past year, you didn't really talk to your family," the chef said, a challenging look in her eyes. "I know that was hard for you. But what if your grandfather doesn't hate every choice you make?"

If Unnon approved of Tom, she had more things to worry about. If she changed her mind and broke up with Tom, Unnon would be angry. If she didn't marry him and start producing great-grandchildren immediately, he'd be angry. She could see that pressure coming down the road. Wonderful.

Then it hit her. Would Unnon's approval itself change her mind about Tom? Maybe if her grandfather and her family actually liked Tom, she'd want him less.

Dani liked to think she wouldn't react that way.

But she wasn't so sure.

THEY DROVE BACK to Monte Verde that night, with containers of cheese, caprese salad, chicken, and *spaghetti alle vongole*. Tom's car would smell like a trattoria for a week.

Milvia had also wrapped up two *sfogliatelle*, exquisite Neapolitan pastries formed of leaves of dough, that Milvia made herself. She knew how much Dani loved them.

Tom was quiet on their drive back up 85, and only answered when she spoke.

"That wasn't as bad as I thought." Dani watched Tom's profile as he drove, highlighted in the lights of a passing car.

"Good. I'm glad," he said. "I really enjoyed myself. That was some of the best food I've ever eaten."

Dani got the feeling he was tiptoeing around something. That he was being careful with his words.

"You and Unnon seemed to get along well tonight."

Tom went quiet again.

"I enjoyed talking to him. I loved hearing about your family. All the traditions, the get-togethers. Oh, God—that story of you talking to your great grandma in fake Italian." He laughed and looked over at her. "I know you have real issues with your family. But you have a close family. They love you in a messed-up way, but they love you. They want to be around you. I didn't have that extended family growing up."

"I think it's hard to know what it's like being in a family, unless you're in that family." Dani looked out the window at lights of houses along the freeway.

"Maybe. But the way you act when you talk about your family worries me," Tom said quietly, as they pulled onto 280 North. "It's not like the Dani I've come to know. I thought if I passed the test tonight, everything would be okay. Now, it's not. Your grandfather had no problems with me. So I'm confused."

"What are you saying? That I wanted you to fail the test?"

"I don't know, Dani," Tom replied calmly. "You have a lot of issues with your family. I'm not sure I can deal with them right now."

She felt impatience building inside her. Did Tom ever get angry? For once, she wanted to hear him yell. Get upset. Then they would fight it out. That was how she dealt with things. It was what she'd learned growing up.

They drove in silence through the darkness in Monte Verde, where streetlights cast pools of yellow light onto the quiet, deserted suburban streets. Soon they reached the rural, hilly part of Monte Verde, and turned onto the road where Tom lived, where the streetlights disappeared. Now it was only house lights, pinpricks of light in the dark far apart from each other, and the glow of the moon above, fighting its way from behind the clouds.

As Tom clicked to open the garage door, she felt deep sadness for the relationship they'd had before anyone had known about it. When it was just the two of them.

Her brother had trolled her, and she'd taken the bait.

Now nothing would ever be the same.

**20**

———

After Reyna got back from the gym that morning, she volunteered to take Jacky to school. She had supplies to drop off at the school, from the PTA's teacher funding program.

Reyna rarely offered to drive Jacky, so Ruiz took her up on it.

He went out to his truck and started it up. He'd end up getting to the station before Grasso. The Winslow case had been circling in his mind since he'd left the station last night.

If Flores had murdered Derrick Winslow, as he thought and hoped, he'd look for more to tie him to the case. So what if he'd gotten to Someplace Bar & Grill by 10:15 that night? He still could have killed Winslow. Aggarwal had said the time of Winslow's death was only an estimate.

They had Flores's fingerprints and his admission that he'd been at Winslow's that night. His statement that he'd been angry at Winslow for stealing his girlfriend. That was more than they had for any other suspect.

Flores was their best bet for an arrest—and a conviction.

Flores could easily have read the details of the Miller case. He'd have known it had taken place not far from Winslow's. There was no witness who could say the house hadn't been robbed after Flores left—only Flores's word that everything was in place when he got there.

One thing had not been found—Winslow's own gun, which had been used to kill him that night. They needed to find that. A complete search had been done of the house and the property. It wasn't there.

Ruiz came in the back door from the lot and stopped by the break room to put the lunch Reyna had made him in the fridge. He filled his coffee mug and sat down at his desk to figure out what to do next.

He wanted to interview Flores himself, but he knew he couldn't—and shouldn't—interview the man himself. But when he found the gun and any other evidence against the man, that would speak for itself.

He began to draw up his plan. Adrenaline purred inside him like a tank of high-performance fuel in his truck. He'd barely touched his coffee, but he felt wide awake. He felt a sureness in him, a growing strength, as if it wasn't his mind putting this together, but his body.

As he placed the call to the judge, his words sounded calm and straightforward. There was cause to believe, based on the questioning of the suspect and the fingerprints, that Mario Flores had killed Derrick Winslow. They needed to find the gun used in the murder.

By the afternoon, he would have the warrant to search Flores's apartment in San Jose.

REYNA STARTED THE CAR.

The Range Rover told her the temperature outside was 36 degrees. Much too cold for California. Too cold for her.

She'd bought the car cheap from one of the patients in the dental office where she worked. She loved how posh she felt in it. It wasn't like the minivans the moms at Jacky's school drove.

After the car had refused to start again, in a bad part of downtown San Jose, Jimmy had finally taken it in for repairs. He'd said he'd never liked the car and was sure the patient had been relieved to get rid of it, but he didn't want to see her in danger like that again. Spending $2,500 on repairs was still cheaper than buying a new car.

Jacky sat squirming in the front seat, his backpack on his lap.

"Mom, may I go to Colin's after school?" He said in his super polite voice, which he used when he really wanted something. "If I skip the afterschool program today, Colin's mom can pick me and Colin up. *Pleeeeease*? We're working on a project."

"A project for school?" She was immediately suspicious because, though the two were best friends, they were not in the same class. Though it was possible all fourth graders had the same assignment.

"We're building a vehicle for hunting extraterrestrials." Jacky said matter-of-factly. "We need to finish soon. It's very important."

"Don't be silly, Jacky." She said, while trying to edge into the traffic on Benton. "I don't mind that you're working on something like that. But your homework comes before anything else. I'll talk to Colin's mom, but you need to finish the homework. She has to agree to that or you're not going."

They paid a lot for Jacky to go to the afterschool program, so she hated for him to miss a day. On the other hand, Colin was a good, smart kid. He would be a good friend for Jacky to have as he continued on to middle school—the time when many kids started to hang out with bad influences. She and Jimmy both had brothers who'd gone off course and started using drugs as teenagers. That would not happen to Jacky. She'd make sure of it.

They pulled up in front of Jacky's school. He slung his backpack over his shoulder, mumbled "Bye, mom," and headed to the line in front of his classroom to join his friends.

She watched him until he was a small figure in the distance. He drove her crazy. She worried about him. And now he and his friend were spending all their time building some kind of crazy machine for hunting aliens. Sometimes *he* felt like an alien to her.

Still, the small bouncing figure in the distance talking to his friends meant more to her than she could ever have imagined.

She headed south on 280 on her way to the dental office in San Jose. Two days till marriage counseling again. She'd agreed to do it after she realized there was no way she could leave Jimmy and live in expensive Silicon Valley on her own. At first, it had been a delaying tactic. Go to counseling for a year or so, until she could afford to leave and be out on her own.

Something changed along the way. Even Jimmy had changed. That was the last thing she'd expected to happen.

When she'd brought up in marriage counseling what had happened to her at the house in East San Jose, that she'd been sexually assaulted by one of the roommates, the counselor said she'd experienced trauma from rape and needed to talk about that separately with another counselor.

She'd found Reyna a counselor she could pay on a sliding scale.

After a few sessions, Reyna saw how much she'd been affected by that event—and by her relationship with Mateo, which the counselor had said was abusive. She didn't have to be treated that way. She realized she'd needed someone to say those words to her.

Even though she wasn't in love with Jimmy, he was kinder to her than anyone she'd ever met. She had friends from high school who were divorced, with three and four kids. One friend who'd died of an overdose. One who'd been stalked and shot by an ex.

Last year she decided to stay where she was. As her counselor had been encouraging her to do, she'd "live in the moment" and see what happened.

Reyna walked in the door of the dental office, later than usual. She could hear Tiff and Alicia laughing in the backroom. The music was on, and the coffee machine hissed and gurgled as it brewed its first pot.

"Good morning, Reyna." Tiny Rocio, the receptionist, smiled from the front desk.

Reyna preferred to come in before anyone else. That way she settled into her day without having to talk to anybody. She prepared her work area and had a cup of coffee by herself before she met with patients.

She was still not on good terms with most of the staff. Rocio was kind to her, never treated her differently after the gossip about her affair went through the office. Dr. Hanford stayed out of it and referred sometimes to the *the women issues* in the office, as if it was a scary place scattered with lady parts that he had no intention of wading into.

Tiff and Alicia had refused to speak to her for months. The girls' nights out they'd had for years had ended, or rather, she was no longer invited. There was no way she'd go running to Dr. Hanford about it. She spent her lunches with Rocio or reading magazines and her nights out with the moms at Jacky's school.

She did her job, cleaning patients' teeth, which she enjoyed. She left it all behind when she got in her car.

There were people she cared about in her life, and she'd save her time for them. As for Tiff and Alicia, she didn't owe them anything. Fuck them.

The same for Mario Flores. She hadn't seen him since the night in downtown San Jose when she'd asked him to come to help her with the Range Rover. Of course, she shouldn't have called him, but she'd missed him. He'd lectured her like he was suddenly a better human being than she was.

As she laid out her tools on the tray, she gave a little snort. Flores didn't even know her. All he knew about women he'd found out in a series of one-night stands. He had no right to tell her what to do with her marriage.

When it came down to it, the things that remained in her life, like the floor beneath her feet, were Jimmy and Jacky. For now, that was enough. The things that happened over the past year, and the things that didn't happen, kept her where she was. It was not as bad as she'd thought.

She'd gradually stopped worrying about where she'd be next year. Or about calculating a move out on her own. At first it had seemed hard, as if she were dumping all her hopes and dreams into the foot-operated trash can in the dental office. Mourning that she had nothing better to look forward to.

But once she'd given them up, she felt lighter and freer.

Maybe this was living in the moment.

GRASSO CRAWLED out of bed feeling headachy and weighed down from last night's dinner.

She decided to skip her run. While Tom slept, she showered and blow-dried her hair. She stood in her robe for a moment at the foot of the bed watching him sleep on his side. His head lay against the white pillowcase, a slight amused smile on his face, even in his sleep. Even Tom's dreams were calm and easygoing.

She wanted to slip off her robe, slide in under the covers next to him, and forget all about last night.

But something shut her down. New questions had moved into her head overnight. She remembered their ride home, the tension between them.

And she couldn't move.

Instead, she went downstairs to the kitchen to find one of the *sfogiatelle* and make some espresso, using Tom's Italian espresso machine. He didn't use it anymore, and it had become a large, fancy kitchen decoration. She'd been fascinated by it and learned to use it by watching YouTube videos. She went through the process, which had become a sweet morning ritual to her, filling a weighty, brown stoneware mug with espresso. After holding the milk pitcher under the steam spout, she spooned out a perfect cloud of white foam over her coffee.

She sat down at the marble island with her breakfast, to go over her notes on Flores's interrogation. She'd typed up a timeline of the day of the murder, based on statements from Justin, his mother, Kira Baker, and Flores.

Then there was Justin's statement, in which he said he'd seen a van parked in front and a man running out to it in the rain late that night. If they could believe Justin, this meant someone had been there after Flores.

Grasso wanted to have something in hand for talking with Ruiz this morning when she went in. In her two years working with him, she'd seen Ruiz's intuition in action. He quickly got a feel for people, for how to reach them, and was skilled at drawing out suspects and witnesses. He usually saw past the bullshit to focus on what was important to solving the case.

His blind spot was huge when it came to Mario Flores. Certainly because of his history with the San Jose Homicide cop. She'd thought Ruiz would be above this. He'd trained her. She respected him more than anyone she knew. This weird position she was in hurt.

She'd talk to Ruiz this morning. Go over the timeline and tell him why she thought they needed to look beyond Flores. Someone who must have come later. Her stomach fluttered with nervous energy, while it continued to process last night's rich, heavy food.

She saved the file and closed her laptop.

Soon she heard Tom's uneven gait coming down the stairs. He entered the kitchen, dressed for a morning of Zoom meetings and calls. A buttoned-down shirt and comfortable, baggy cargo pants.

"Good morning." He said, his face almost expressionless, as if he was thinking of something else. "I thought you'd be gone already. You didn't run?"

She shook her head. "All that food last night. Everything. I'm not feeling great."

He scratched his head and took a seat across from her. "Yeah, I know what you mean."

"And last night was—" Her throat felt thick, swollen. "Maybe we can talk about it later."

He looked serious, his brow furrowed, and his head tilted. She wondered if this was his management look. The way he looked when he was considering a decision at work, one that would affect the many people who reported to him.

"Dani. I was wondering if it might be a good idea for us to take a break. Everything has happened so fast—you moving in over the past six months. All that's happened with your family. It might be good for us to have some time apart. I think you should go back to your place for a while."

Suddenly her chest began to tighten. She couldn't breathe. *What the fuck was this?*

"I-I'm—" She was ready to start in on an explanation of what she'd said on the ride home, then pride choked her words. She stiffened.

"Fine. I'll come back at lunch to get my things together." She closed her laptop. "I'll go back to the condo after work."

"I might not get to see you." At least she saw some regret in his face. "I've got budget meetings. I'll be in my office for most of the day."

Tom watched her with a strange look on his face. She couldn't read it. She wished she'd seen something: sadness, kindness, affection. She didn't see any of those things.

She shoved her laptop and printouts in her bag and gulped down the rest of the coffee. She'd lost her appetite for the *sfogliatelle*. She opened the waste basket under the sink and dropped it in.

Then she slung the bag over her shoulder and grabbed her purse, while he stood at the counter, looking like he was about to say something.

She gave him some time.

When he didn't say anything, she left.

**21**

———

Grasso got into the MVPD detective room, feeling weak and shaky. Coffee wasn't going to help with that, so she filled her water bottle at the cooler instead.

Ruiz was on the phone, standing next to his desk.

She turned around to see him watching her at the cooler. Once she'd filled the bottle, she motioned him to call her. He nodded.

As she sat down to go through her messages, her throat constricted with pent up sobs. She sure as hell wasn't going to let them out here.

It would be really nice if Tom had called after she'd left and told her: *On second thought, let's keep things the way they are. Come back tonight. We'll talk about it.*

There was no such message on her voicemail. She was wondering if he'd been right. Maybe they did need a break.

The phone rang. Ruiz spoke quickly and abruptly.

"Schallert wants an update. Five minutes. See you there."

She didn't want to bring up her thoughts about Flores

before talking to Ruiz first. But this was a high-profile case. Of course, Schallert would want a status update.

She gathered up her printouts and headed for the sergeant's office, where Ruiz sat.

Schallert closed the door and took his seat. Meetings with the older, white-haired Schallert were usually a pleasant chat, with words of fatherly encouragement. By the look on the sergeant's face, that wouldn't be the case today.

"Jimmy, Dani. I hear there's been some developments in the Winslow case. I'm getting a lot of questions from the community. With the Miller case still on people's minds, it's a public safety issue. We need to put this one to bed."

"We've come to the conclusion that this was intended to look like a copycat of the Miller case." Ruiz took out photos of Winslow's house and passed them to Schallert, who began looking through them. The ransacked office, the walls stripped of art, cables dangling from holes in the wall. The photo of Derrick Winslow in his bed.

"Anyone who lived here would remember the details of the case." Ruiz pulled out a report from the original case. "And anyone with access to police databases would know the details."

Schallert nodded. "So you're saying someone tried to pin Winslow's murder on the unknown assailants at the Miller house. But Winslow was the actual target."

"Yes, sergeant," Grasso said. "Winslow's house is a few blocks away from the Millers' house. We think whoever killed Winslow was taking advantage of that to make it look like another home invasion."

"Fine. You've got suspects?" Schallert sat back in his seat, his arms crossed. "We need to make an arrest soon. I've got realtors on my back. Who wants to pay $8 million for a house in a neighborhood with a history of violent home invasions?"

"We've made progress," Ruiz said firmly. "Crime scene says the murder weapon was probably Winslow's SIG Sauer, which has been missing. I just got approval for a search warrant for one of the suspects."

Grasso quickly turned to look at Ruiz. This was news to her. He'd done this without her, and she knew whose property was going to be searched.

"We'll be searching the apartment of Mario Flores, detective with San Jose PD Homicide." Ruiz continued. "Love triangle situation. He had a motive. His fingerprints were found on the scene. He admitted he was at Winslow's that night and left at 10."

"A detective." Schallert stroked his white mustache and looked thoughtful. "Interesting. I'm sure there's a story there, but I want to see an arrest soon." His voice turned stern. "Got it? You two keep me updated."

Side by side, she and Ruiz walked out. When they were a distance away from the sergeant's office, she turned to him.

"So you put in for a search warrant for Flores."

"Yeah." He looked down at his coffee mug, avoiding her eyes. "It's approved. We'll search his apartment in San Jose later this afternoon."

"You didn't say anything to me about this. Why? I let Flores go. I believed him, and the prints made sense with his story. We need to talk to Justin again."

"Let's talk outside." Ruiz said gruffly, as heads in the station lifted up from their work, all eyes on them.

They turned left out of the station and walked toward the residential streets outside of downtown. Replays of her morning conversation with Tom intruded on Grasso's thoughts, but the cold slap of wind on her face kept her focused.

"Justin Winslow has been in psychiatric care for the past two days." Ruiz said as they walked. "His statement isn't going to hold up—"

"We can at least investigate it—ask if neighbors saw the van."

"It's half a block between houses up there, Dani. You think someone would see that on a deserted street at 10:30 p.m.? Or somehow get a plate number?"

"Flores was upfront with us. He told us exactly where he went in the house. The owner of Someplace said he showed up when he said he did."

Ruiz studied her face. He snorted. "Flores has an affect even on you, Dani. I thought you were better than that."

She was ready to be angry. To lay into him with her suspicions about his motivations, but she remembered what he'd been through the past year.

"I know you're angry at him, Jimmy, and you have a right to be. You need to make sure you're being honest with yourself."

"We need to make an arrest." Ruiz was walking faster than she was, and she was struggling to keep up with her shorter legs. They passed a house, where a grey-haired woman working on her roses watched them with interest. "You heard Schallert. Flores is our suspect. You shouldn't have let him go."

"You're the only one who can know—" She felt like she was screaming it into the wind. "—whether you're doing this to get back at him or not."

Ruiz stopped at the end of the street, and she caught up. He looked down at her and his face softened.

"Dani, I should have let you know about the warrant. I was afraid of you stopping me."

*That should have been a clue. What you're doing is wrong.*

They walked around the block, till they got back onto Main Street heading back toward the station.

They went around to the back entrance through the car lot without saying much and headed for their desks. Ruiz seemed hard at work and didn't look up once in the next forty minutes.

Grasso prepared herself for moving out of her boyfriend's house during her lunch hour.

And for searching an apartment she didn't think needed to be searched.

GRASSO PARKED on the road in front of Tom's house.

Tom's tenants were outside weeding a garden plot in front of their small house on the slope behind Tom's house. Carrie and Bart Angwin were always friendly to her and made sure she got a sample of anything they grew or baked. They were sweet hippie vegans, not much older than she was.

Grasso opened the front door, which Tom rarely locked. She'd warned him about that many times in the past few months.

In the front hallway, she heard him in his office a few rooms way, talking loudly in an online meeting with his department at Infinitas.

She was relieved that he was busy. She could gather her things and leave without any interaction with him.

In the bedroom, he'd made the bed and picked up a shirt, bra, and leggings she'd left on the floor and folded them and laid them on her dresser in the closet. Another difference between them. He kept a neat, orderly house. She left clothes and dishes all over her apartment and had relied on the cleaning crew to whisk it away for her when they came at the end of the week.

She pulled over a stepstool next to the closet and stood on it to reach up and pull down her big suitcase.

She threw in the contents of her dresser drawers, then her black dress and heavy jacket from the closet. She jammed her toiletries from the bathroom into the zippered inner pocket of the case.

Tom's voice echoed down the hallway as she made her way downstairs with the suitcase.

"Ted, what are your priorities for Q3?" Tom was asking someone in the meeting. As long as he kept talking, Dani felt at ease. She didn't want to run into him. She hoped he didn't know she was there.

Now she'd need something to put her PlayStation in. She rooted through the kitchen drawers till she found a box of large black trash bags. Not elegant, but it would work. She pulled out a few and headed for the living room.

She wrapped a bag around the console to protect it, then put it into another bag, along with the two controllers. She coiled the cables and slipped them in.

Tom's voice continued to echo from down the hall.

"Human Resources won't need that," she heard Tom say. "Go ahead and strike that line in the budget."

She glanced around and didn't see anything else she needed. They'd spent so much time in this room. Gaming, making out. Binge-watching episodes of their favorite shows while eating take-out food.

Bags in hand, she walked back to the dining area off the kitchen, with its French doors that opened out onto the deck. She'd miss having breakfast on the deck, where she'd watched the deer approach gingerly like women on high heels. They were beautiful, even if Tom's neighbors complained they were an invasive species. She loved to watch the hummingbirds hover, almost effortlessly, over the Mexican sage plants.

She knew she was stalling. She needed to get out. She carried the bags out to the car first, then came back for her suitcase.

She was loaded up, and with one last look at Tom's house, she drove back to the station.

**22**

———

By late afternoon, dusk descended on San Jose. Grasso and Ruiz drove, without speaking to each other, down Lincoln Avenue in the Willow Glen neighborhood. It was a homey small town tucked into in a very large city, and Grasso saw why people liked it.

It was quainter than downtown Monte Verde. Mothers pushed strollers down the sidewalk. People walked their dogs, who stopped to lap from water bowls in front of some of the stores. She counted a few coffee shops, several restaurants for foodies, and an antique store.

Flores's apartment building, around the corner on Willow, was painted retro pink and grey, and probably built in the 1950s or 1960s. Ruiz pulled into the spot closest to the upstairs unit Flores lived in.

When they reached his corner unit, Ruiz rapped on the door. After some delay, Flores opened the door, his face white. Before him stood a pissed-off Ruiz, holding a warrant to search his apartment for a murder weapon.

Flores stood there, apparently dressed down after a day

of work, wearing something he probably wouldn't want to be seen in public in: a t-shirt with bleach stains and ripped jeans that hung loosely on his frame.

When Ruiz showed him the warrant, Flores stepped back and let them enter. A crime scene tech followed behind. Flores stood awkwardly in his kitchen drinking a lemon Pellegrino and scrolling through his phone while they went through the apartment, room by room.

She and Ruiz spent most of their time in the bedroom, looking through drawers, under furniture and in the closet. Grasso noted that Flores had an incredible amount of navy-blue suits—and more of those flashy expensive ties that looked so un-coplike.

She looked through the shoe rack on the floor of his closet, which held rows of Flores's impressive collection of shoes, for almost any occasion: retro wing tips, topsiders, dress shoes, hiking boots, and about five pairs of sneakers, including running shoes and colored Converse high tops.

She took out the running shoes, which she recognized as high-end Nikes. She pulled out the tongue to check. Size 8.

"Jimmy, look at this." She showed him.

He raised his eyebrows and grinned. "Big surprise."

In the nightstand next to his bed, Ruiz had found a small gun safe.

"Flores," Ruiz barked out. "We need you to come in here and open this."

"It's my piece for work," Flores came in from the kitchen. He typed in the keycode to open the small safe. Ruiz had brought a photo of Winslow's gun, a SIG Sauer, and this Glock looked nothing like it.

Rummaging through his top dresser drawer, Grasso found a boudoir-style photo of Kira Baker. Kira wore a pink ruffly negligee that revealed a lot of cleavage. Cherry red lipstick covered her half-open lips. She looked like the airbrushed, carefully curled version of the woman she'd interviewed the day before, but with a porn star vibe.

What did men see in a woman who looked like this? Smooth and fluffed up like a cone of cotton candy. Cotton candy with boobs. She just didn't get it.

They spent two hours going through the small apartment. When they found nothing relating to the case, Ruiz asked to see Flores's Prius, which was parked downstairs. He and the crime scene guy went down to go through it.

She waited upstairs in Flores's apartment, taking the time to check her text messages. For anything from Tom. Nothing.

Detective Mario Flores stood in his kitchen, a haunted look in his eyes.

"I'm trying not to take this personally." Flores swallowed and smiled weakly. He put the phone down and leaned against the counter, his arms crossed. His eyes said he desperately wanted them to be gone.

Grasso felt the urge to defend Ruiz, even though she was pretty sure it *was* personal, at least part of it.

"You know how this works, Flores. You were there the night Winslow was killed. You're a suspect."

Flores blinked. "Yeah. Add it to the list of my fuckups."

He was generating enough pity for himself without any from her, though she was sad for him. "Mario, I've heard you're a smart guy. Maybe think with your brain and not your penis." She was shocked at the words as they came out of her mouth but didn't regret them. After the stress of today, she'd lost her filter.

Flores laughed, the nervous laugh of someone who hoped he'd be off the hook soon.

"I have a sister. Dawn. You remind me of her, Grasso. She's my conscience."

"Maybe you should call her next time you feel like doing something stupid."

She heard Ruiz's footsteps coming up the stairs. By the look on his face, he hadn't found the gun. Flores turned away from her and started loading glasses and plates into his dishwasher.

When Ruiz came in, Flores stopped and stared at him.

"Jimmy." Flores said it sadly. Like he wanted to start some conversation. One look at Ruiz, and Grasso knew that wasn't going to happen.

"Ready to head back?" Ruiz smiled and nodded at her. He ignored Flores, who turned back to the sink, shoulders slumping as he continued rinsing dishes.

"I FOUND Winslow's address scrawled on a post-it, under the front seat," Ruiz said as he backed out of the parking spot and eased the car onto Lincoln Avenue. "That and a napkin from Someplace B&G with a phone number on it. I'm sure he's got a big stack of those."

"No sign of the gun."

"If he's got it, it's not on his property." Ruiz sounded disappointed. "He's a detective. I'm sure he put a lot of thought into disposing it where it couldn't be found."

That night after wrapping up at the station, Dani went home to the condo in Cupertino. She hadn't stayed there in close to two months.

When she opened the door, the heavy scent of cleaning

fluids hit her—bleach and lemon-scented sprays. It looked new. Counters clear. Fridge completely empty. Dust wiped off the blinds. Like a show home. A place no one lived in.

After months at Tom's, her place looked tiny. The rooms seemed small. There was no forest or deer outside the door.

The cleaners had continued to come every week. If she'd cancelled, her mother would have heard about it and started asking why.

Grasso ordered pizza, an afterwork ritual she'd actually missed since moving in with Tom. She lugged the trash bags with her PlayStation in from her car and sat cross-legged on the floor as she reconnected the console. After rebooting her wi-fi, she was up and running.

While she waited for the pizza delivery, she did twenty minutes on her treadmill, then checked her phone. No messages from Tom.

She felt some nostalgia being back in her condo. Pizza and a game, her nightly tradition. She could even go back to playing *Sands of Illustra*. She wouldn't have to wait for Tom to find time to play with her.

Dani started up the PlayStation and considered going back to one of her older games. Why not go with the nostalgia, as long as she'd been dumped back into her old lifestyle. But she couldn't find anything that interested her. She did check to see if Tom had logged onto PlayStation. He wasn't online tonight.

She looked out her large full-length window at the lights of the valley. In the distance, to the west, she saw the dim lights of Monte Verde at the base of the mountains.

The scent of bleach and antiseptic emptiness made her open the window for a few minutes.

When the pizza arrived, she took out a paper plate and piled on a couple of pieces. She rooted through her cabinets and found a bottle of red wine, a Grasso's Fine Foods special red blend. She opened it and ran it through an aerator, then poured herself a nice big glass.

She carried her dinner over to her big, overstuffed chair. The cleaners had folded her down comforter and put it in the bedroom, draped across the foot of the bed. She dragged it into the living room like a toddler with a security blanket and made a nest of the chair.

She ate pizza and drank wine while she watched video game play-through videos, which served as background noise more than anything else. She ate four slices of pizza and drank three big glasses of wine one after the other without thinking. It was like her body kept screaming for more and could not be satisfied.

She must have dozed off, because at 2 a.m., she woke up, disoriented. She turned to her side and realized there was no warm body next to her.

She was in a chair, not a bed.

She cried until her comforter was damp with tears.

FLORES WALKED into Homicide the next morning in his best navy suit, with a striped tie his mom had bought at Harrods in London.

He heard Dawn's snarky voice again, as he imagined her watching him.

*Feeling down this morning? I don't blame you, Ro. That was a hell of a surprise last night. Maybe Ruiz was targeting you. Maybe not. Can you say you didn't deserve it?*

*You went with the stockbroker look this morning, like you always do when you're feeling like shit. Hey, whatever gives you the confidence to keep going.*

He sat down at his desk and ran through his calendar.

Today at 10, he was supposed to meet with Buckley about leading a team again.

Of course it would be *today*. Fuck.

After a gulp of coffee, he typed up some talking points on his phone. He should be fine. He'd have to hope that word hadn't gotten back to Buckley about the search. Or about the fact that MVPD had questioned him in the murder of Derrick Winslow.

He met Buckley in his office at 10, as confident a smile on his face as he could manage. Buckley waved him inside and seemed happy to see him, which was a good sign.

"Flores, come on in. Have a seat."

He took a seat in front of Buckley's desk, his heart pounding in his chest. He took a deep breath, trying to focus and slow it down.

"Well, I've got a case for you. Just came up. A homicide up on Communications Hill. It looks like a domestic case. Everyone else is working the double murder in North San Jose. It's you, Roberson, and Dirkson."

Flores felt like getting up and doing some Roberson-style dance moves till he heard that last name. Mandy wouldn't be excited about this. He'd be surprised if she would submit to his leadership without complaining to Buckley and trying to get out of it. But it was a start. Roberson was one of the most ADHD cops he'd ever worked with, but he was confident that with some structure, they could handle this together.

"I'm on it." Flores gave the sergeant what he hoped was a relaxed smile, as a cascade of fireworks went off in his stomach. "You won't regret this."

Buckley nodded distractedly. "The trafficking case. The

girl's murder. Jesus, that story broke my heart. Quick thinking on your part, Flores."

"It was disturbing," Flores said. "After I saw her, all I wanted was to find that guy." Which was true. The only thing that enabled him to be okay that night was the fact that the Highway Patrol had taken Ronald J. Perez into custody down south.

"Keep it up, Mario." Buckley looked at him with encouragement with a little condescension. "Don't lose focus. Slow down and tell me what you're doing, so I know I can trust you."

"Thanks, Sergeant."

He left the office feeling better. He just had to hope and pray that Buckley, or anyone else, didn't hear about the Winslow case. As long as Ruiz and Grasso arrested someone else, he was home free.

Now to pin down Roberson before he got his sugary treats at the vending machine.

Then figure out how to win Mandy back to his team.

And pray Ruiz wouldn't have him arrested.

MANDY SAT at a table in the break room, eating her lunch while she pored over an article in a magazine. Now was his chance. He needed to talk to her, but he dreaded it. She could throw a lot in his face and probably would, judging by her reactions to him lately. She wasn't speaking to him; she'd gotten back to Roberson and not him with her search results in the Fuentes case.

He'd dealt with a lot of shit this past year, so what was a little more? And what didn't kill you made you stronger, according to Nietzsche and Kelly Clarkson.

"Mind if I have a seat?" He put on his best smile and started to pull out a chair.

She shot him a disdainful look and went back to her article, tucking her red hair behind her ear. "There are other open tables in the room."

"Mandy, I need to talk to you. Buckley put you on my team for the Communications Hill murder. We need to get on this. You, Roberson, and me. The three of us need to meet in a half an hour." He wasn't going to give her an out.

"Wonderful." She looked up at him. "I get to work with the guy who flaked on the job last year, the guy I had to cover up for consistently. The guy who was out screwing some other cop's wife instead of doing his job."

So that was as expected. But Flores knew he deserved it.

"Mandy, I have no excuse. I messed up. You went above and beyond with the Schuler case, and you filled in when I flaked out. I owe you a lot."

Mandy just stared at him. She threw up a hand. "Okay."

"Buckley put you on my team, and I'm glad. I am fortunate to have you and Roberson after what I did."

Mandy glared at him. "Do you understand that I've worked harder than you, worked here longer than you and I've never gotten the opportunities you've gotten? You come to me when you need information or help, then you scamper off to solve your case and get your pats on the head."

"Mandy, I'm sorry—"

"Not interested in your apologies. Here's the deal, Flores." Mandy began. "I'll work with you. But I want to be recognized for my work. Jesperson is slow and meticulous, but he gives people credit. Tries to promote his team. You need to learn from that. Don't make it about yourself."

Flores hadn't expected this response.

"Fine." He sighed. "I'll see you in a half hour. I know I've got a lot to learn."

Mandy sat there, staring at him. When he got up and pushed his chair back, she was still staring at him.

Flores walked away, knowing that what he'd been given today was good. This wasn't going to be easy.

But it was only going to work if Ruiz didn't arrest him for Derrick Winslow's murder.

**23**

———————

Grasso woke up in the chair, the comforter twisted around her, in hangover hell.

Her head pounded. Her stomach felt bloated.

She grabbed her phone to check the time. She'd forgotten to set her alarm. It was 6:15 a.m.

She did a quick message check. Nothing from Tom.

If she got up now, she'd have time for a run at Rancho. She wasn't sure she could get up and do that without throwing up, but she could try. She needed her morning runs. They regulated her, so when she got to work, she was focused and settled.

If there was a day she needed a run, it was today.

Fifteen minutes later, she was dressed in shorts, a t-shirt, and a hoodie, driving down Stevens Creek Blvd to Rancho San Antonio Nature Preserve, a popular running and hiking spot in the coastal hills.

She grabbed a spot in the parking lot, which was easier to find on these cold winter early mornings. She twisted her earbuds into her ears, turned on her running music and headed up the hill.

As she ran up the trail, her head ached, and her stomach warned her that it wasn't happy with the last two nights of heavy food. She stopped at the edge of the path and felt like she was going to be sick. After a rest and a gulp or two of water, she continued.

After that, she fell into her usual rhythm. Soon she was moving up the zig zags through the hills. She sucked in the cold air and found herself waking up.

The rising sun was brushing the hills with orange light, and her body shivered with the pleasure of starting her day in this beautiful place. As she started her descent down the hill, she felt that freedom again—that she was somehow flying. Plunging down the hill, abandoning herself to gravity.

Back at the trail head, she stretched. It was only then that she started to think about Tom. How she wanted to bring him here when his leg healed up, so he could see the morning sky, and maybe feel the exhilaration of a run himself, once his leg was ready for more intense exercise.

She wanted to hear from him. She wanted to text or call him. But then, he'd suggested the break, not her.

As she pressed her leg against the stretching bars, she wondered how she'd managed to turn a perfectly good evening with Unnon—an unexpected success really—into such a fucking mess.

"Can we walk today. Please, Papa?"

Jacky was dressed and ready for school and was bouncing around in the doorway with a little too much energy and excitement.

Ruiz rolled over and sat up on the edge of the bed. He

rubbed his eyes. He hadn't slept well last night, with Schallert's warning that they needed to make an arrest soon. He'd also been thinking of Flores. For the first time in a year, he'd actually seen him. It had made him feel good that Flores looked scared shitless.

"Sure, *mijo*." Ruiz stood up and went to set out clothes for the day before he showered. "Get some breakfast."

"Mom said I could have toast and grape jelly." He said solemnly. That didn't sound at all like something health-conscious Reyna would say, but he wasn't going to fight it.

"Go make it yourself. I gotta get ready."

In a few minutes they were at the door, and Jacky was trying to lug his backpack, full of books, over his shoulder, while grasping the strange, misshapen object in the black garbage bag.

"Can I help you with that?" Ruiz reached down to pick it up.

"No! Don't touch it," Jacky screamed so loudly, Ruiz started to worry.

"*Mijo*, what's in the bag?" Ruiz demanded. He wasn't sure what it could be, but his mind went to every possibility. He'd grown up with a younger brother who'd started getting in trouble at the age of 11, not much older than Jacky.

Please let this not be anything he'd stolen. Something he wasn't supposed to take to school. Pornography. Drugs.

Jacky's eyes filled with tears. "But I don't want you to see it."

Ruiz bent down and looked at his son's face. He saw shame. Embarrassment.

"Jacky, show me."

"You'll laugh." The boy shook his head. "Mom thought it was silly."

"I won't. But I need to see it."

"It's something Colin and I work on when I'm at his house on Thursday nights, when you guys go out. I invented it."

He opened the bag and took out a large box, painted bright green. There was a tube set in the end. Taped firmly inside was a battery-operated airbed pump from an inflatable mattress they'd had that died years ago.

"Colin and I are hunting extraterrestrials. I made this device that captures them. See?" Jacky flipped a switch inside the box and put his hand over the tube to show the sucking effect. "We see any, we suck them right up. Then we'll keep them in cages so we can study them for scientific purposes."

Ruiz kept a straight face. "I see."

Jacky was different than his brother or Reyna's brother had been at this age. Jacky was more likely to end up addicted to video games and superhero and sci-fi movies than drugs. Maybe he should have trusted his instincts.

"You've done a good job with this, *mijo*. Thanks for showing it to me. I'm happy to help you carry it."

Jacky put the device back in the bag and handed it to him seriously, as if he were placing in his hands the prototype of some new tech invention.

With utmost care, Ruiz lifted it and held it firmly, and they headed out the door to school.

Grasso was in Cupertino, and it was only 5:30 p.m. As she sat in her parking spot in front of a boba tea place finishing her drink, she didn't feel like going back to her condo yet. She wasn't the same person she was six months ago, and the condo was no longer her burrow, a cozy place to hole up with pizza and games and escape the world. The thought of going back there depressed her.

An idea came to her, probably because she was filled with frustration—at Ruiz, the Winslow case, and her family.

Alex and Anthony worked two miles away, at Grasso's Fine Foods HQ, on Saratoga-Sunnyvale Road in Saratoga. She'd call them and tell them she wanted to meet. For the past few weeks, they'd treated her like an eight-year-old—someone they could taunt and threaten whenever they felt like it. This was going to stop.

She called Anthony's cell phone. He probably hadn't looked at the caller ID. He answered in his usual low, sluggish tone.

"Grasso's Fine Foods, Saratoga. Anthony Grasso speaking. How may I help you?"

"It's Dani. Your sister. I need to talk to you and Alex. *Now*. I'm nearby. Let's do this."

Long pause. "Hey, Dani. What's crackin'? This is short notice. I don't think I can—I mean, we have a meeting with Unnon in fifteen minutes—"

"You know what, Anthony?" She said with a force in her voice she didn't remember using on anyone, even in interrogations. "Tell him you'll be fucking late. I want you and Alex to meet me behind the Starbucks across from Grasso's. We're going to talk."

Anthony didn't have a comeback for that and just let out a long, exasperated *fine*.

She started up her car to drive past the endless strip malls and restaurants on De Anza Boulevard, which turned into Saratoga-Sunnyvale Road once she crossed into Saratoga. Even with traffic, it would take her ten minutes. She had no guarantee either of them would show up. But it felt good to know she'd scared the crap out of

Anthony, and that he was probably on the phone to Alex right now.

She pulled her car into the shopping center parking lot and made her way to the end, to the Starbucks, a hangout for local high schoolers. She wheeled the Mini Cooper around the back of the coffee place and parked where she could easily be seen by anyone looking.

She turned off the engine and waited. She checked her messages for anything from Tom or Ruiz, who was still on his Flores rampage.

Still no word back from Marcia Winslow Davies about the possibility of talking to Justin again.

When the last rays of sun faded into darkness behind the hills, she realized she'd been here twenty minutes. It looked like Giovanni Grasso had won out.

As she prepared to start her car, she saw headlights coming toward her. A black Tesla, which she recognized as Alex's, rolled to a stop next to her. The window rolled down and Alex popped his head out.

"My car has more room than yours." He looked at his watch. "Get in and let's make this quick. We told Unnon we'd be back in fifteen minutes."

"I get shotgun," Grasso called out before she got out of her car. "I'll take the time I need. You'll just have to deal with it."

Anthony rolled down the window and whined.

"No way." He crossed his arms over his seatbelt and stayed firmly anchored in the passenger seat. "You're my little sister. You've never gotten shotgun, and you're not gonna start now. Get in the back."

"Get out, Anthony. Or I'll tell Lara you let the kids stay up till 11 when she's away."

Anthony swore under his breath and got out of the front

passenger seat. He made a big show of moving to the backseat.

Grasso slid into the front seat.

"First of all, yes, I have a boyfriend. Second of all, it's none of your fucking business if I want to hold hands with him or kiss him in public. Yeah, we had dinner with Unnon, and he met Tom. But I don't want every little thing about our relationship broadcast to the whole family."

Alex turned to her, a look of fear on his face. "But Dani, we're so happy for you."

"Yeah, we are," Anthony piped up from the backseat.

"Why did you threaten that you were going to tell everybody in the family about Tom if I didn't bring him to a family dinner?"

Alex turned around and glared at Anthony. "Jesus. You didn't tell me you said that."

Anthony crossed his arms and gave them both a sulky look. "I just wanted everyone to meet him, that's all."

Grasso turned around and looked at Anthony then Alex.

"I am 25 years old. I'm not eight. If you wanted that to happen, you could have just asked. Don't threaten me. It's not your job to *force* me to introduce Tom to the family. Do you even get what I'm saying?"

Alex nodded. Anthony mumbled a weak, "yeah."

"I was treated like I wasn't part of the family for almost a year," Grasso said. "During that time, I learned how to live without you guys, even though I missed you so much. But if you threaten me or treat me like an eight-year-old again, you're not going to see me. And it will be my decision this time."

Alex reached across to hug her. Anthony reached his hand up from the back seat.

"Dani." Alex squeezed her. His eyes were watery. "You've

put up with a lot of shit. I can't guarantee you won't have any more of that from our family. I mean, it's our family, right? But I'll do my best to make sure it doesn't happen. I know I've been busy with Arlo but talk to me if you're being treated badly. Will you please?"

She wrapped her arms around her older brother and hugged him for a good long time. "I think I can do that."

**24**

———

That last morning, several hours after they'd taken his body away, Olga Kostenko had gone upstairs to the computer in Derrick Winslow's office. She'd been in there earlier in the week, while Winslow was downstairs in bed with the big lip girl.

She'd learned his passwords by watching him enter them. She knew the code for his safe.

As always, she was invisible. She could enter a room unnoticed, stand and watch him log on, then act as if she were picking up dirty coffee cups to take downstairs or bringing in an extra ream of paper for the printer.

That day, she sat down in his big leather chair and read through the emails again. Along with the letters Mr. Winslow had planned to send to GrowGo's board members and international network of specialists, and to the management teams of the startups on GrowGo's roster.

She'd learned the details of Winslow's plan—to destroy a man's reputation, in stages, over time. With cold, calculated, and timed releases of lies that could turn a person from a respected tech professional to someone who wouldn't be able to find a job anywhere, ever again. It might even cause his family to doubt what they knew to be true.

The plan would start by planting the tiniest seeds of distrust. Bringing up times he'd given incorrect information, so he started to feel unsure of himself and began making mistakes. Questioning his integrity in front of others. Making sure information that the startups needed from him was lost. Giving wrong instructions to software development in his name. Even feeding tips to the technology press that his credentials were forged. Starting rumors that he could be a pedophile.

Slowly this person's reputation would be beyond saving. Winslow would write to the board telling them the only wise course of action was to get rid of him. It was for the good of the company that he be let go.

Then Derrick Winslow would take full control of GrowGo.

Olga had thought for a long time about her decision.

As she sat with mama in the early evening, when the old woman started to get her night confusion, she would hold her cold hand in hers and think of what to do.

Olga didn't like to think of it in those terms, but there was good, and there was evil in the world.

The problem with that was, there was usually good and evil mixed up in every person. She had never thought that she would see a person who was completely evil. But after seeing The Plan, she knew she had.

She would change sides. Give her loyalty to someone else. Not because they were more powerful than Winslow. But because the evil she'd seen from Winslow had filled her with that much disgust. She'd learned this new thing about herself: she was willing to risk what she had to stop something evil.

She printed the emails and letters. She wrapped them up in a box for him to pick up and take home after a meeting with Winslow early that week. She left the box under the back deck, as they'd agreed upon.

Early on the day Winslow was killed, the person called to thank her. Olga asked if she could be paid something for her trouble. She was paid very well.

Again, she was paid for her silence.

By the next morning, Winslow was dead.

AFTER DROPPING Jacky and his ET device off at school, Ruiz hit heavy traffic crossing the valley and pulled into the station's back lot twenty minutes late. He slammed the door of his truck in frustration and hurried in the back entrance.

He and Grasso needed to talk, but he wasn't excited about it.

The gun hadn't been found. At Flores's apartment or in his car.

Flores was their best bet for an arrest right now. They could bring him back for an interrogation, questioning him more specifically on his actions that night. Ruiz wanted to question Flores himself, rattle him into revealing more about that night, but knew he shouldn't.

He pinged Grasso shortly after he got in.

Meet me in interrogation. Let's talk about next steps.

Sure. 5 mins

THEY MET WITH THEIR BREAKFAST. Grasso was eating a muffin with her coffee. Or rather, she was picking pieces off it listlessly with her fingers and leaving them in a pile on the paper plate. She seemed tired.

"We need to rethink things," Ruiz said as Grasso took a sip of coffee.

"Sure." She said, wearily. "Why don't you tell me what *you* think we should do next, Jimmy."

"Flores was there, close enough to the time of death and we have proof. His size 8 shoes match the tracks in the carpet. The guy had a motive. We need to do it."

Grasso looked weary. "And you're okay with not following up with what Justin saw that night? The guy running out to the van at 10:45 p.m. If Flores did this, where are the pieces of art? The TV and the devices that were stolen? They weren't at Flores's place or in his car."

"Flores is smart enough to figure out how to get rid of these things." Ruiz sat back in his chair. "We need to bring him back for another interrogation. I want to grill him, and based on his answers, we should be prepared to make an arrest."

"Fine," she threw up her hands. "But while we're at it, Jimmy, I want to see if I can talk to Justin Winslow. His mom says he's coming home from the facility tomorrow."

She couldn't let go of what Justin had seen that night.

"You go set that up, Dani. I'm going to get Flores back in here."

Ruiz studied her face. She was mad that he'd bypassed her on the search warrant. That must be it. She looked upset, like she'd been crying.

"I know you think I went behind your back on the search warrant—"

"You did. But you don't seem to get this. You *want* Flores

to be guilty. And now Schallert wants an arrest to keep the realtors happy, so he's made it a done deal."

GRASSO CALLED Marcia Winslow Davies's number. The ringtone continued four times, then she left a message after the tone for her to call back.

If Justin could somehow identify or describe the van, that would help. If he could describe the man running for it, that would be even better.

But Justin was just coming off two days in a mental health facility. If there was a way to get more information out of the student, without causing him more stress and confusion, she wanted to do it.

Around 10 a.m., Grasso got a call back from Marcia Winslow Davies. Justin was home, doing much better, and she recommended that today would be a good time to talk to him.

"We were hoping, though," Marcia said, her voice low, "if it could just be you coming, Dani. You're younger and—female. Justin's been very sensitive to men, because of his experience with his dad."

Grasso could understand this. She did feel obligated to tell Ruiz—and told him on her way out of the station.

On her way, she heard her phone receive a text. At a stop sign, she glanced down. Tom. Her heart began pounding.

She needed to wait till this was over to read it. Reading anything from him would throw her focus off.

In fifteen minutes, she was on the doorstep of the Davies' home on Waverly Street in Palo Alto. It was a large, two-story home with natural wood siding, large, mullioned windows, and green shutters. It looked like the house Anne of Green Gables would live in, if she decided to relocate to Northern California.

"Detective, please come in," Marcia greeted her. "I don't think you've met my husband Kenneth yet, Justin's stepfather."

"Good afternoon, Detective Grasso." Kenneth, a man with clear eyeglass frames and graying hair. He did not look happy that she was there.

Then he turned to Marcia, hissing under his breath, though Grasso could hear him. "We do *not* need this right now, Marcia. This is a bad idea."

Marcia widened her eyes at her husband as if to say *not now*. "He'll be fine, Ken."

Grasso felt like she was seeing a behind-the-scenes glimpse of the Davies's life, which seemed to revolve around Justin and his needs. For a moment she wondered what lengths Marcia and Kenneth would go to in order to ensure Justin's well-being.

She wondered if they would be willing to kill to do away with the source of the teenager's pain.

Marcia led her down a long hallway, over a bright black, green and yellow Persian rug. She tapped on the door at the end of the hall. No Joker picture on this door, Grasso noted. Justin called for her to come in.

When she opened the door, Grasso was surprised to see Justin looking down at her from the top of a large loft bed, under which stood a desk and chair and bookshelves stuffed with books. A red electric guitar sat on a stand next to the desk.

There were two other large bookcases, also filled with books. Grasso wanted to look through them, since she liked to learn about people from the books they chose to read. Justin would be an interesting young man to figure out.

"Hello, Dani." Justin smiled, which seemed like a positive start. With his hair combed, he looked even more like the photos of his father. She wondered if he was still happy about the fact that his father was dead. She hoped his therapy sessions had helped him come to terms with the fact that he hadn't killed him.

It was odd to interview him when he sat on the loft bed, higher than she was. But he seemed comfortable and at ease there.

When Marcia Davies left, Grasso took a seat on the overstuffed chair across from the bed.

"You look a lot better than when I saw you last, Justin. I'm glad to see that." Grasso sat back in the chair and looked up at him. "Do you know why I'm here?"

Justin's legs dangled down from his bed. He looked more like nine than nineteen.

"My mom said you wanted to ask me some questions about that night." Without the agitation of his time at the station, his voice sounded completely different. He didn't look scared or angry.

"You talked in our interview a few days ago about something you saw the night of your dad's death. You said you saw someone run out of the house on Maldonado. You remember that?"

"I did see someone," Justin said calmly. "It was before I drove away. A person. A guy, I think. Anyway, he was running out to a van parked on the street. He was carrying an armful of stuff."

"Can you tell me what he looked like? It would be helpful."

Justin closed his eyes, as if visualizing the scene that night. "He was not super tall. Wore glasses, I think. He wore a big raincoat."

"Do you remember anything about the van, Justin?"

"It was in the street, parked aways from my car. On the other side of the driveway entrance."

"You wouldn't happen to have seen a license plate on the van, would you?"

Justin smiled softly, as if remembering something from his past. "If I did see it, I would have totally memorized it. I do that with things. License plates. Random numbers I see. The decimal places for Pi. It's fun for me. I think it's an autistic thing."

Was it that he'd been too emotional that night of his arrest to focus? These descriptions seemed precise and detailed.

"Thanks for your help, Justin. I really appreciate it."

With Justin's info, Grasso left and headed out to her car.

She'd call Ruiz after she took a moment to check the text.

She took a deep breath. She wasn't sure what to expect.

She tapped to open her messages. When she saw Tom's words, she started sobbing.

> We shall return to fight as partners ere the
> suns of Azir rise.

৯৯

With Grasso in Palo Alto talking to Justin Winslow, Ruiz mapped out his plans to arrest Mario Flores.

The ideal would be to go to his workplace. To arrest him in front of his fellow detectives and his sergeant. Everyone would crane their necks to see it. People would come out of their offices to watch Flores walk out in shame.

He pictured the look on Flores's face when he and

Grasso showed up. When they read him his rights, just as Flores had done on so many of his own arrests.

Ruiz had listened to Grasso's and Ladera's interrogation of Flores. It had been hard for Ruiz to hear his voice again. He didn't believe a word the detective had said.

But there was one part that Ruiz related to in Flores's testimony.

Flores had said the only thing he had left was his job, and he didn't want to lose it. Ruiz remembered feeling that way, too. Last year when he'd found out Reyna was planning to leave him. He remembered what it had felt like to know he still had his job. He could come into the station in the morning and see people he cared about and who cared about him—Grasso, Ladera, Dawson, McConaughy, and Schallert.

He decided he could not take that away from Flores. Flores had gotten himself into this situation. But he could not put him through that shame, in the one place that made a difference for him.

He'd be kind. He would not arrest him at work.

**25**

———

Beth Fisk watched the numbers on the gas pump roll over then finally stop. A full tank. That was the problem with living in the boonies. You had to pay big bucks to gas up your car in order to drive anywhere. And this morning she'd have at least an hour's drive.

She replaced the pump and got in her car, with a cup of cheap gas station coffee, loaded up with powdered creamer, in the cupholder.

Michael had been worrying her again. You'd think he'd be happy once Winslow, the source of all evil, was dead. But that was not turning out to be the case, and now she had an idea of why. So when Michael got up early at 5:30 to go into the office, she'd called in for a substitute teacher this morning, saying she'd caught something. She'd had a lesson plan and an activity for the kidlets in her desk. With some quick instructions to the sub, she was set.

Weekday traffic on all the freeways she had to cover had turned out to be horrendous. It was almost an hour and a half before she reached 380, the crossover to Highway 101. Then it would be a quick run to the exit she'd take.

Once she got to the complex, she parked in one of the resident spots—feeling guilty that she couldn't find a visitor spot. But who the hell was going to dole out parking citations on a weekday morning? Almost anyone who worked would be on the freeways already.

She looked up the phone number, which she'd copied from Michael's phone. Money must be a big deal to this woman, so she'd use that. Offer to pay her off for what she knew if she'd just come downstairs to meet her. Beth glanced around the small, shabby complex and spotted a row of dumpsters on the side. Perfect.

The woman picked up the call on the third ring.

"I'd like to pay you for some information. Meet me by the dumpster on the side of the apartments. Please come by yourself."

At first the woman gave her some bullshit about not wanting to leave her mother by herself. But after a pause of a few seconds, she agreed to come down and meet her.

She saw the woman making her way down the external stairs from the second floor, a wiry woman about her age, with a head of greying blonde hair. She was dressed in an oversized blue sweater and was still wearing a pair of slippers. For a moment Beth felt a twinge of pity so strong she was tempted to leave and drive home.

Then it hit her. If she didn't deal with this now, it would blow up into a bigger problem. What she was about to do was necessary. You didn't solve problems by ignoring them. Michael liked to do that, and where had that gotten him?

The handgun was in the glove compartment. She hadn't shot in a few years, but she knew how to use it. Her father had taught her at a shooting range outside of Sacramento when she was a teenager. It had been one of their better times together. Her father told her it was a good thing to keep around, and he said he'd rest easier, now that she had a gun and knew how to use it.

The woman was heading for the side of the complex. It was time, and Beth knew she couldn't delay.

She slipped the gun into her purse and opened the car door. Then with firm, quiet steps, she made her way to the side of the complex.

It was noon. Grasso wasn't back yet.

Ruiz decided to walk down to Garcia's and get himself a burrito. It wasn't something he usually did by himself.

He considered asking Ladera to join him, but the guy was in the break room going over the plays of last night's Sharks game with a couple of the younger patrol officers. Ladera was laughing and talking up a storm. Ruiz wasn't going to interrupt that.

At Garcia's, David Garcia asked him why he was by himself and quickly made up his regular order. When it turned out to be colder outside than he thought, Ruiz decided to bring his lunch back to his truck.

Marriage counseling was coming up again tomorrow night, with all the fears he usually associated with it. Last week's session had been good, but this week's subject—he and Reyna's physical relationship—terrified him.

He didn't feel like mingling today. He'd eat his burrito in the peace of his truck, then get back to work.

He opened the door of the truck, settled himself in the seat and plunged a straw into his diet soda.

Then when he reached down for his burrito, he felt a hand reach out from the jump seat behind him and grab his shoulder.

**26**

---

"**P**ut the fucking food down."

The voice sounded hoarse but familiar. Ruiz blinked his eyes and tried to focus.

*Calm down. Let the guy talk.*

The more he talked, the quicker he'd be able to identify him.

Ruiz set the burrito down on the dashboard and held his hands up to show he had no intention of using his weapon. His heart pounded like he'd just run a mile.

Then he remembered. When he'd pulled into his parking spot this morning, twenty minutes late, he'd hurried inside without locking his truck.

He didn't know who this person was or why he was in his truck. Was he armed? He angled his head as slowly as he could, trying to get more of a visual. He wondered how quickly he could get his gun out without getting killed.

"Don't ruin my fucking life." The voice continued, hoarse and distorted. "I didn't murder Derrick Winslow. Yeah, I went to his house that night. I wanted to know who my girlfriend was seeing. Winslow hit me, then I left, just as I said in my interview. I didn't want to lose my job."

"Mario." Ruiz dropped his hands. He should have known.

"Grasso and that older guy, Ladera, let me go. They didn't see a reason to keep me. So why are *you* doing this to me? The search warrant. Jesus. Like I had his gun. If you would have just asked me, I would have let you into my apartment to look anytime, no judge required."

"Mario, you were in the house the night Winslow was killed. Your fingerprints on the wall outside the office prove it. The tracks in the carpet match your shoe size." Ruiz spoke the words as he looked out his windshield, waiting for someone to come out so he could call for help. He wasn't sure what Flores would do in his current state.

Now Flores was quiet. Ruiz looked into his rear-view mirror and saw the detective. There were circles under his eyes, and his skin looked pale and pasty.

"I should have apologized, Jimmy. I was in a daze back then. I didn't fully realize what I'd done to you. I had an affair with your wife. I don't know if you can believe me, but I wanted to be your friend when we got together at Someplace Bar and Grill. I respected you so much. I looked up to you. I still do."

"Bullshit," Ruiz said under his breath. Flores was desperate. He'd say anything to avoid arrest.

"What I did cost me. I don't know if you realize that. I lost my position in the department because I wasn't doing my job. I can't excuse what I did. It was my fault. I've spent the past year trying to make it up." His voice became muffled. In the rearview mirror, Ruiz saw Flores in the small seat in the back, his head in his hands.

Ruiz spat out the words. "You wanted to be my friend, so

you had sex with my wife? That doesn't make any sense, Flores. All of this went on behind my back. We worked together to find Schuler's killer, and all the time you were having an affair with Reyna. You talk about trying to make it all up, but I've spent the past year in marriage counseling. I'm busting my ass to fix something I didn't even break—"

Ruiz stopped himself, realizing that wasn't really true. He was learning that. He closed his eyes and threw his head back against the headrest

"Flores, get the fuck up here." Ruiz sighed. "I'm not gonna keep twisting my head to talk to you."

Flores opened the back door and got out, then slid into the front passenger seat.

He and Flores talked for about forty-five minutes. He saw Grasso parking, then she got out and passed them on her way into the station. She gave Ruiz a questioning look. He waved her on.

"I'd do anything to erase that week from my life, Jimmy." Flores said at one point. "I'm so sorry. Can you forgive me?"

What a weird word that was. It reminded Ruiz of Sunday school lessons when he was a kid. What he'd gotten out of it, with his kid brain was, *Somebody did something bad to you. Now be nice and forgive them.* At that time, he could nod to his Sunday school teacher and say, *yes, I forgive my little brother for stealing my change jar.* Beyond that it was hard to wrap his head around it. His father had complicated things; if Manuel Ruiz showed up at his door, he would never forgive him for what he'd done to his mother. He would not be nice.

He could not pretend Flores hadn't done what he did.

But he would like to be free from the anger, all the obsessive thoughts that had filled his head since he'd found out about the affair. He'd been living in a hell and for the past year Flores had sat upon the throne there. Flores didn't deserve all the space in his head.

It wasn't as hard to forgive Reyna for what she'd done, but he saw her every day—it was easier somehow. It was harder to forgive someone you didn't see. Someone at a safe distance you could pinpoint as the source of all your troubles.

"I don't think I can forgive you, Flores."

"I wish we could sit down and have a beer together at Someplace." Flores sighed. "Do you think that will ever happen?"

Ruiz couldn't picture it happening. But he wasn't feeling threatened by Flores. Reyna had said she wanted nothing to do with Flores. Ruiz felt sorry for the guy. He knew Flores had been trying hard not to be his father's son, while doing much of the same things his father had done.

When Ruiz looked at the clock in the dashboard, he saw that it was 2:15 p.m.

"Well, I gotta get back inside."

"If you're going to arrest me, do it now, Jimmy." Flores was almost daring him; he didn't want to go back into limbo. He wanted to know his fate. "But do it because you think I killed Winslow."

Ruiz's phone rang. Grasso's ring tone. The ring intruded into his thoughts, reminding him of where he was and what else he had going on today with the case.

He answered and heard Grasso's breathless voice.

"Jimmy, Olga Kostenko's been shot outside her apartment complex. She's in critical condition at Sequoia Hospital."

## 27

Ruiz quickly dismissed Flores, telling him not to leave the area. He would call him back later.

With an odd look at Ruiz, Grasso climbed into the passenger seat for the trip to the hospital in Redwood City.

"Want to tell me why you were talking to Mario Flores in your truck?" Grasso asked. "I kept coming out back to check you were still there. I was worried about you."

Ruiz took the exit for El Monte Avenue.

"We had some business to settle," he said gruffly. "He scared the hell out of me. He got into my truck's back seat, and that was my own damn fault. After talking with him, I'm not sure he killed Winslow."

Grasso didn't say anything, but he could feel her relief. She had a faint smile on her face.

Grasso told Ruiz about her talk with Justin Winslow.

"Justin was very different today." Grasso gripped the armrest as Ruiz sped north on 280. "Calm. Focused. It might have been because of his new medication. If so, hurray for meds. He told me what he'd seen, in detail. Kenneth Davies did not want me to talk to Justin. He was trying to get Marcia Davies to send me away."

"So what did the kid see?" Ruiz rubbed his face. He was emotionally exhausted from his discussion in the truck.

"Justin saw a man on the shorter side, wearing glasses and a big floppy raincoat, running out to a van parked on the street. He was carrying a bunch of stuff, as Justin said. He said the time was around 10:45 p.m."

"Fisk? Or Flores. Both are around 5'6." Both wear size eight shoes." Ruiz sighed. "Did we get phone records for Winslow's landline?"

"Yeah. Why?"

"I want to confirm something. I got a call back from Conor Doyle in Ireland."

"Want me to see if Ladera can look it up and get back to us?" Grasso asked.

"I need to know if there was an international call placed the night of Winslow's death around 10:30 from Winslow's landline."

Grasso put in a call to Ladera, who began searching the records.

Ten minutes later, as they approached the exit for the hospital, Ladera called back. Ruiz tapped to put it on speaker phone.

"Hey, guys. I found it. There was a call made from Winslow's line to Dublin, Ireland at 10:32 p.m.," Ladera said. "Duration 22 minutes."

"Ladera, you rock," Grasso called to the detective, before Ruiz hit to end the call.

"Conor Doyle remembered something. He was confused at first as to who was calling him that night. It was supposed to be Michael Fisk, to give him software support. But the display read Derrick Winslow."

Ruiz saw the next exit, Woodside Road. "Fisk wasn't at home. He was at Winslow's that night. He must have come right after Flores. He made the tech support call shortly after he killed Winslow."

Ruiz turned to Grasso. "Let's head back to Monte Verde to make an arrest. And throw up a prayer that Olga Kostenko survives."

"Agreed." Grasso nodded.

Ruiz pulled off at Woodside and got on the entrance for 280 south to head back to Monte Verde.

AT 3:30 they parked behind GrowGo's Monte Verde headquarters. The place looked quiet, with only one car in the parking slots. With caution, Ruiz went around to the front entrance of the building, followed by Grasso. He kept his hand near his gun.

Grasso opened the front door, and they walked in. Acoustic guitar music was playing, a hipper, more chill equivalent of muzak.

Other than that, the reception area of the business looked deserted. Framed logos from GrowGo's many startups filled the walls of the reception room, probably for the purpose of getting potential entrepreneurs excited about joining a startup with the potential to *disrupt* the tech marketplace. This was the dream—to join a startup that became a new and profitable leader in technology, an app on everyone's phones. Or a household name like Amazon or Facebook.

The office seemed empty, Ruiz and Grasso prepared themselves, in the event that Michael Fisk was here.

"Monte Verde Police. Come out now with your hands on your heads."

Silence. Soon they heard footsteps. Slow and hesitant.

From one of the offices, a young man with a blond beard came out, his hands raised and a look of terror on his face. It wasn't somebody Ruiz recognized.

"We're looking for Michael Fisk." Ruiz said bluntly, while scanning the room. "Is he here?"

The young man kept his hands up. He began to babble, nervously.

"Michael was here about an hour ago. I've been here since lunch, and he left right after I came in. He said he was going over to Derrick Winslow's house. I-I'm Kent Culver. I work for Sparkville, one of GrowGo's startups." He looked lost and scared. Like he'd stumbled into a situation far beyond his experience and knew it. "I flew in this morning from Austin because Michael was going to give me a product demo and introduce me to the development team. But when I got here, he took off and said he'd be back."

Fisk had probably driven up to Redwood City to shoot Olga Kostenko. Maybe she'd been talking about how Winslow's character assassination of Fisk had led to murder. Maybe she'd known what he'd done and had been blackmailing him.

"Kent, you should leave and head back to your hotel until you hear more information from somebody at GrowGo," Ruiz said firmly to the young man, who looked confused and a little sad. "You're not going to have your meeting today."

In a daze, Kent Culver opened his messenger bag on one of the desks and put away his laptop. He took one last look around, then hurried toward the back door.

Ruiz alerted MVPD to send patrols to GrowGo

headquarters in case Fisk came back. And to send backup to Winslow's house on Maldonado.

He nodded to Grasso, and they headed for the car.

By the time they got up to Winslow's house, the sky had darkened, as if getting ready for an early dusk. It was only 4 p.m. The trees at the end of the street rustled and shifted, as if nervously awaiting the confrontation to come.

At they turned onto Maldonado, where the street connected with Folsom, Ruiz saw patrol cars lined up. They weren't visible from Winslow's, but they sat there, ready.

Winslow's house looked quiet. No lights on. Fisk's car, a Lexus, was in the driveway. The only movement visible at the front of the house was the wind rustling the tiny leaves on the Japanese maple. Ruiz's stomach tightened.

"Let's go inside."

Grasso nodded.

They parked under a tree, two houses down from Winslow's. Ruiz saw the curtains part in the house's window.

He and Grasso worked their way along the curb, trying to stay out of view of Winslow's house.

They finally reached the house, and Ruiz motioned to the side yard. There were no fences here, and Ruiz remembered that there was an entrance on the side leading to a large bathroom with a jacuzzi. A smooth stone path led from the door to the back of the house where there was a stone-inlaid area with a fire pit.

Grasso followed him up to the door. Ruiz tried it, but it was locked.

Grasso pointed to the back. "Master bedroom door," she whispered in his ear.

They crept along the side of the house toward the back as the sky grew darker. Grasso nearly tripped on a rake camouflaged under a pile of leaves, but she steadied herself. Had Fisk heard the rustling noise? They waited for a few minutes. No sound from the house.

They approached the back of the house. In the dim light, it looked empty. The deck was deserted, white folding chairs arranged in a circle as if for a group meeting that never happened.

The back lights suddenly came on, covering the deck and back lawn with blaring light. Ruiz heard Grasso take a sudden breath. They'd probably been triggered by light sensors. Or by Fisk, trying to scare the shit out of them.

The sliding glass door to the master bedroom was right next to them. The lights were not on in the room. Ruiz saw the dark outlines of a bed and a dresser.

The lever for the door was in the down position. Unlocked.

*Stay*, he whispered in Grasso's ear.

He moved along the door, trying to cushion his steps, keeping his feet as light on the boards of the deck as possible to avoid creaking.

He pulled the handle back and the door slowly slid open.

He slipped into the darkness of Winslow's bedroom.

Once inside, Ruiz's eyes adjusted to the light. The bedroom door to the hallway was closed. He had some time to think this through. He tried to picture the layout of the house, from the night of the home invasion-murder. There were three bedrooms on this level, two bathrooms, then the kitchen, a large great room where Winslow held meetings, a dining room and a laundry/mud room between the garage and the kitchen. Upstairs—Winslow's office, three more bedrooms and at least two bathrooms.

If Fisk was here by himself, Ruiz guessed he'd be in Winslow's office.

He opened the door to the hallway and listened. He heard a printer upstairs, shuttling out paper. He crept out into the hallway, making his way toward the floating stairs.

Ruiz was still in the hallway when he heard a noise. Quiet grunting.

He crept back to the kitchen, on his right. There on the floor lay Jeff Gabbard, bound and gagged.

## 28

Ruiz took out his pocketknife and cut the ties on Gabbard's hands and feet, then cut away the gag. Gabbard gasped and Ruiz quickly put his hand over the man's mouth. Then he put his finger to his lips.

Gabbard nodded. He stood up slowly and winced as he stretched his legs.

Ruiz pointed down the hallway. Slowly and quietly, Gabbard headed back down the hallway toward the master bedroom. Outside, Grasso should have been communicating with the backups by now. They were prepared to advance, so if Fisk found him—or shot him—it wouldn't be long before they were in.

The printer stopped.

Ruiz no longer had the cover of that noise. He tried to put himself in Fisk's place. What would he do next? If he'd shot Olga, he must be desperate. She must have known he'd killed Winslow and she'd threatened to tell someone. Like Flores an hour ago, he might be bold, thinking what the hell, he had nothing to lose at this point.

Ruiz didn't want to face a trapped, angry Michael Fisk

armed with Winslow's gun, but he didn't think he had a choice right now.

The stupid floating steps. The only way to get up to the office.

He crouched and began making his way up them. Upstairs, Fisk cleared his throat. The nearness of it filled Ruiz with fear.

He took the next step and the steps' iron support vibrated long and loudly. *Fuck.*

Ruiz heard movement in the office, then the loud squeak of an office chair turning. Instinct told him to do it while Fisk was still surprised—Ruiz ran. Up the steps and across the hall runner carpet. He dove into a bedroom, where he crawled on the floor to the other side of a bed. He lay there as still as he could.

He heard footsteps, then Michael Fisk's voice.

"Who are you? Who the hell is here?"

The voice became distant as Fisk went down the hall, looking into rooms. Then when he turned in the other direction and came back, he sounded closer and closer.

"So it's Jimmy Ruiz."

Around the corner of the bed, Ruiz saw Fisk's face in the hall. Pale, sunken. His eyes behind his clear-framed glasses looked abnormally large. In a flash of movement, he saw the gun he was carrying. A SIG Sauer.

"Jimmy, I know you're in here. Tiny Grasso wouldn't make that much noise."

As Fisk walked passed the doorway to the bedroom, Ruiz lifted his gun and shot. He grazed Fisk's forearm. The man wailed, then came in and pointed the gun at him.

"Get up, Ruiz. Looks like you released my hostage. Now it's your turn."

❧

OUTSIDE IT HAD STARTED to rain. The wind whipped through the trees behind the house. Drops of cold rain stung Grasso's face.

Suddenly Grasso saw Jeff Gabbard stumble out of the sliding glass door, red marks on his wrists. His legs looked stiff and bent, like he'd been tied up for some time.

She held his arm to guide him to the side of the house, where the patrol officers waited.

"Fisk is in the office upstairs. I came by after lunch and he was going through Winslow's papers. He threatened me and tied me up. He's got a gun. Not sure where Ruiz is, but he's going for Fisk."

Suddenly, a gun shot rang out from upstairs.

Grasso's heart sank. She prayed it was Ruiz shooting.

*Please, keep him safe.*

Quietly, she entered the sliding glass door. She waved to the two patrol guys, McConaughy and Rogers, and they followed.

They moved quickly down the hall and paused when they reached the stairs.

Michael Fisk was talking loudly upstairs, and it must have been to Ruiz.

"It was self-defense. Winslow was going to kill me. He'd already started."

"Rogers—McConaughy," She turned to whisper to the two patrol officers. "Can you record this?"

She heard Ruiz's voice. "Michael, what do you mean Derrick was going to kill you?"

"He had a plan to kill my career. To get me out of GrowGo, so he could take over. It's right here—the plan." She heard papers shuffling. "You can read it if you like. He had already started the campaign. Like a campaign to market a product, but in this case, it was a systematic plan to discredit me. To destroy my reputation with disinformation. He'd arrange for meetings to be changed and not tell me. He made sure crucial shipments I'd promised would not arrive on time. He'd tell people I'd said something when I had not. The worst was a series of media posts with faked photos of me at a strip club—which took a lot of explaining to my wife and even then, I'm not sure she believed my side of it. I would never do something like that."

"When did you find out, Michael?"

"I found out last week. First, I saw the strip club photo Winslow posted on Twitter, on some guy's account, which I'm sure was fake. A bunch of tech bloggers retweeted it. That's when I suspected what was going on. Olga Kostenko printed out the plan Derrick had written up and left it for me under the back deck. I was shocked that she'd pass it on to me—she seemed loyal to Derrick."

"Why didn't you go to the police?" Ruiz sounded sympathetic. "Why didn't you tell us?"

"Do you think anyone would believe me? It sounds like insanity. Or like the ravings of someone who's jealous of their successful partner. I'm sure Derrick planned it that way. If I tried to tell anyone about it, I would come off looking paranoid."

"Isn't that better than a murder charge?"

They heard sobbing. "You don't understand. Winslow was *evil*. Not just to me."

She heard Ruiz's voice, like a father calming his son. "Yes, I know. Justin Winslow, Marcia Davies, Natalie Chen."

"I had to stop him." Fisk was continuing to sob. "I defended him for so long. All I got in return was bullying. Everything he did was for his own benefit. Even helping companies through GrowGo. When one of our startups sold, he got a huge percentage of the sale, which I didn't realize till recently. It was built into the contract as entrepreneur training fees."

Grasso began making her way up the stairs, stepping lightly so she wouldn't start the stairs vibrating. McConaughy and Rogers followed carefully in her wake.

Ruiz continued asking questions, calmly drawing answers out of Fisk. He was doing a great job of stalling the killer.

"Why did you plan the murder to look like the Millers' home invasion?"

"I remembered hearing about it when it happened. Such a shocking event to happen in this town—and unsolved, too. When I was thinking about how to kill Derrick, I went back to read up on the case in local newspaper archives to get the details. It would be a good cover. An attack not far from the first one." Fisk's eyes lit up as he explained his research. "Did you know that if you walk back into the forest behind this house, there's a short cut to the Millers' house? It's unbelievably close."

Grasso and the patrol officers reached the top of the stairs and moved into position in the hall, a few feet away from the bedroom door.

Ruiz continued to engage Fisk.

"Michael, if you received all of this helpful information from Olga Kostenko, why did you shoot her this morning?"

There was a long pause in the conversation.

"Michael?" Ruiz's voice.

"I didn't shoot Olga Kostenko."

*uck,* Grasso thought. If it wasn't Michael Fisk, who'd shot her?

Grasso moved closer to the opening of the door. She saw Michael Fisk walking back and forth in front of Ruiz, who lay along the edge of the bed, his eyes looking up at Fisk. Fisk looked confused. Olga's shooting had thrown him off. His eyes were troubled as he tried to figure this out. It made no sense to him.

"Why would I shoot her? She told me what Derrick was doing to me."

Grasso saw that Ruiz had taken advantage of Fisk's confusion to shift his position. He moved closer to the door. He was now within striking range of Fisk.

"Michael, did you tell anybody that you'd talked with Olga?"

Fisk stood for a moment, thinking. Then his face twisted into a look of horror. His words came out softly, trailing off.

"Oh, God." He looked dazed. "I told Beth."

Grasso's eyes locked onto Ruiz's. He nodded.

Grasso rushed in, followed by McConaughy and Rogers.

Rogers tackled Fisk, who fell on his side on the floor. While Rogers tried to hold Fisk down, Ruiz tried to wrestle the gun away from Fisk.

There was a gunshot. Then another.

Rogers leaped back, and McConaughy reached in to grab the gun.

Ruiz rolled over on his back, blood draining fast from a hole in his side. Now Grasso saw Ruiz's gun, on the other side of him, next to the bed. He hadn't gotten a chance to use it in the struggle.

Michael Fisk lay on the floor, a shot through his chest.

Two more patrol offices came in, then EMTs. In a whirlwind of activity that Grasso's mind was having a hard time following, Fisk was declared dead.

A stretcher came in and Ruiz was lifted onto it. Grasso felt sick when she saw that his eyes were closed. The paramedics trundled him down the stairs.

A couple of minutes later, Grasso heard sirens and the sound of tires rolling on wet pavement, as the ambulance headed off into the night, its siren growing weaker and weaker in the distance.

GRASSO SAT BACK on her heels and cried. She wasn't aware of anything around her now, only that Ruiz was gone. There was blood all over the floor, blood on her shoes, her slacks.

Rogers and McConaughy helped her up and led her out of the room and downstairs. Rogers hugged her.

They took her into the kitchen and let her wash her hands and gave her a glass of cold water from the refrigerator door.

"Drink it." McConaughy watched her as she gulped down the water. "That's it. Now take a deep breath, Dani."

"Ruiz. He's not dead," she said when she'd finished. "He's not. Is he?"

McConaughy and Rogers exchanged looks. "We don't know yet. He took a big hit in his side, but at least it wasn't in the chest like Fisk."

"Who shot?" She rubbed her head, which ached. "I couldn't tell."

"I checked Ruiz's gun," McConaughy said soberly. "He fired once—I think that first shot we heard from the bedroom."

Fisk must have shot himself and Ruiz. Whether either of those shots were an accident, she didn't know.

Guilt filled her now. Had this been the last time she'd see Ruiz? She'd been angry, frustrated at him for insisting Flores had to be guilty of Winslow's death. She hadn't had a civil conversation with Ruiz in several days. He never told her exactly what he and Flores had discussed in his truck.

She needed to call Reyna. The woman had never been one of her favorite people, but she was Jimmy's wife and needed to know what had happened.

She pulled out her phone and called.

"Reyna, Jimmy's been shot. The ambulance just took him."

Reyna cried out. "Oh, God. Where are they taking him?"

"Probably Stanford. I'll find out and get back to you."

"Dani, I'm going to call now. I'll find him. Thank you."

After Grasso hung up, she felt dizzy. She went back to fill up her glass of water and stood at the sink drinking it down.

In the entry way, Aggarwal had just arrived. Grasso walked up the stairs with the examiner, telling him what she'd seen.

After his examination, he told her that with the wound Fisk had, his death had been quick.

She asked him about Ruiz's wound, describing it as best she could. A gunshot to his lower left side and what that would do. Was it survivable? Aggarwal said it was hard to say, but from what she described, if he received immediate medical care, he had a good chance of survival.

Grasso knew there would be questions about what happened, and they'd have to sit down with a committee to figure out the sequence of events in Fisk's death.

It was necessary, but right now all she wanted was to go home.

Wherever that was.

**30**

———

She finally walked out the front door of Winslow's at 7:30 p.m., after Aggarwal had left and Fisk had been taken away, after all the photos were taken, and the crime scene team had swarmed the place like bugs, busy retrieving bits of evidence that could be formed into a case, an explanation of what had happened tonight in Winslow's house.

It was bleak and dark on the lightless street, and the wind was still whipping the rain into sheets. Ruiz's truck was still parked a few yards away. Seeing it sent a pang through her chest.

She saw another car, parked a few feet back from it. Someone was in it, but it was dark and she couldn't see much.

She stood in the driveway, looking out at the bleak night, her head pounding, trying to remember details of today so she could go back and document everything. Rogers walked out and asked if she needed a ride back to the station.

She was about to say "yes" when the door of the unidentified car opened.

When she saw his face, she ran, without a thought of the rain or what Rogers would think—what Tom would think—and Tom opened his warm arms to her, his face damp with rain.

He whispered to her. "Let's go home."

In the morning, the Redwood City police arrested Beth Fisk in the shooting of Olga Kostenko.

Olga was making a slow recovery but was expected to live. She'd identified Beth Fisk as the one who'd shot her—to keep her from telling the police. Olga had given Michael Fisk the documents that had driven him to murder.

Olga's sister Anya told Grasso that Fisk had written her sister a check for $50,000, for "helping him out."

"My sister has strange ways of thinking sometimes," Anya said, as she fluffed up her mother's pillow on the hospital bed that took up much of the Kostenko's dining room. "She suddenly decided Michael Fisk deserved her help. And that the man she worked for was evil. Still I am not understanding all of it. But we have some money now."

Ruiz had surgery overnight but was expected to be released in three days. When Grasso visited him, he was starting to get grouchy, which she told him had to be a good sign.

"You're getting back to your old self, and that makes me happy."

As he talked, he said he thought Fisk had tried to kill himself—and accidentally shot him, too. "I was collateral damage," Ruiz said with a sad smile. "Once he figured out his wife had tried to kill Olga Kostenko, Fisk gave up."

On his second day in the hospital, Ruiz received a visitor.

Detective Mario Flores entered at the beginning of visitor's hours. Ruiz had had a weird dream about him visiting that night before, so it was startling to see the guy actually walk into his room as he'd appeared in his dream: in his fancy-ass navy blue suit.

"So-Cal kid," Ruiz gave him a mock frown as he entered.

"I felt the need to dress up," Flores smiled. "I'm heading up a case now."

Flores gave him a brief overview of the Communications Hill murder case.

"You're not a bad detective, Mario. When you're paying attention."

"Thank you—I guess?" Flores laughed. "There's still one person on the team who's not thrilled to be working with me. I can understand why."

It could have been the discussion in the truck. It could have been because Ruiz had been shot and faced the possibility of death. But Ruiz's hatred of Flores was slowly draining away. Maybe he was in the process of forgiving the guy. Or more likely, with his injury and painkillers, he didn't have the energy to maintain his anger.

"So, Jimmy," Flores said. "When you're okay to drink beer again, can we go to Someplace?"

*Jesus.* Flores had asked this before, like a kid relentlessly bugging his parents for candy or fast food. Going to Someplace was Flores's way of resetting their friendship. Rewinding to a time before he'd made one of the biggest mistakes of his life. Where he'd perpetrated a home invasion of his own.

"Give me some time to heal up, and I'll think about it."

Flores brightened like a Christmas tree.

## 31

Two months later, Ruiz drove up Maldonado and parked in front of Winslow's empty house.

He remembered Michael Fisk saying there was a quick route through the forest, from Winslow's house to the Millers'. Ruiz walked to the back of Winslow's property, to the stand of dark, shuffling trees that had looked so ominous the night Winslow had been murdered.

Then Ruiz turned left and walked along the edge of the forest, along the backs of the large tracts of land and their sprawling custom houses. Houses that people like the Grasso family could afford to live in. Where the Ruiz family could never afford to live.

Soon he was near the end of Folsom Road, where the Millers had lived. Near Justin and Marcia Winslow Davies's former house.

The ghosts were still with him. He remembered that night at the house on Folsom, its images so horrific and vivid in his mind. The bodies he'd seen, of the family that used to sit down and have dinner together. A home destroyed. He saw them in his dreams, but not as much as he used to. Sometimes they returned to him, reminding him that there were still no answers.

He saw the high fence and huge new home built after the Millers' home had been bulldozed. A sprawling pink stucco building, bloated and ugly, with balconies everywhere.

When he looked to his right, he saw there was still some debris from the destruction. Rotted boards and concrete chunks, pushed beyond the lot's boundary line into the trees to get them out of sight. Weeds and a few tree seedlings had begun to reclaim it.

He circled the pile, then picked up a stick to poke at it. When he saw something that looked like cloth, he nudged at it with a stick. It looked like t-shirt fabric. The sun had bleached exposed parts of the black shirt to light gray.

When he lifted the tattered cloth with the stick, he saw something smooth and greyish-white. At first, he thought it was a smooth stick, stripped of bark. Then it hit him, right in the stomach.

*This is a bone.*

And only because he'd happened to see one in person before, at a forensics class, he thought it looked like it could be a *radius*—a bone in the forearm that curved into a kind of cup at the end, to join with the ulna make up the elbow. This didn't look like an animal bone.

He took a photo of it on his phone from a few different angles, but he was careful not to move it. He circled the pile and bent down to see if he could spot any more. A painful tug in his side reminded him that his body was still healing from the gunshot and surgery, and he shouldn't be doing this. He spotted another bone, this one shorter.

He called the station.

Within 45 minutes, Andrew Rogers came out with a

young woman, an osteology expert from the county forensics team.

"Janine here says you took the winning picture." Rogers joked. "What the fuck are you doing out here anyway, Ruiz?"

Janine Chai looked up from the bones, which she'd carefully arranged on a mat set up on a small folding table. "Nice find, Detective Ruiz. I could tell from the photo these are human. And pretty recent. We'll test these at the lab to figure out the victim's age then test for DNA."

The next day, Rogers called Ruiz to say a forensics team came to the site to sift through the rubble. They found more arm and leg bones and skull fragments. After the discovery, the remains stayed at the forensics lab for two months, as higher priority projects pushed them farther down the queue.

Justice, like forgiveness, can take some time.

Ruiz decided to bug the lab with a few phone calls over the next month, reminding them that this discovery could help solve Monte Verde's most notorious cold murder case.

Through DNA testing and with the help of a genealogical service, the forensics team finally determined the bones belonged to 32-year-old Dennis Campion, a convicted felon who'd disappeared five years ago. Ruiz discovered that two of Campion's friends—Jason Esposito and Charles McComber—were now in prison for a home invasion in Southern California.

The most likely scenario was that Esposito and McComber killed Campion and left him to die in the crawlspace of the Miller's home. Wood splinters were found among the skull fragments, and Ruiz remembered the baseball bat on the floor of the Millers' bedroom.

Esposito and McComber now faced other charges, including four murders. Detective Daley in Marin County was ready to launch an investigation into the possibility that the men had also robbed Oscar Williams's home in Mill Valley.

Ruiz knew now what had happened that night on Folsom Road.

It would not bring back the Millers.

But the ghosts in his head were free.

ONE OF THE good things about his injury, Ruiz thought, was that he got to miss marriage counseling for three whole weeks.

After his release, he was on medical leave and spent most of his time watching movies and reading through a box of thrillers and mysteries Tom and Grasso had brought over with a really good Italian dinner.

By the time the three weeks were up, it was a sign of his boredom level that Ruiz was excited at the prospect of leaving the house, even if it meant going to counseling.

"I'm driving this week." Reyna had a look of concern on her face as she pulled the keys to the Range Rover out of her purse. "The doctor said you should avoid any strain to your side for two months."

Ruiz hated the Range Rover as if it were his mortal enemy, but he knew the car was important to Reyna.

"Sure, that's fine, babe." She'd been driving Jacky to school and picking him up for the past three weeks. She'd taken on his wound care, changing his dressings and taking him to checkups. She'd been friendly and sociable to everyone who'd dropped by with meals. Ladera, McConaughy and Rogers brought take-out burgers and stayed to watch a Warriors game. Colin's mom dropped off an Indian dinner with homemade *naan* that was better than anything he'd had at an Indian restaurant.

Flores was not one of the visitors, but they had a date set next month when they'd meet up at Someplace for drinks.

"You two have been through a lot together."

In Ruiz's opinion, Jennifer de Groot, LMFT, looked very pleased with herself.

"Reyna and Jimmy, this past month has been quite a test. Rather than pick up with our topic of your physical relationship, I'd like to open this up to you. What have you learned during this time? About each other? About yourselves?"

Ruiz was relieved at the change of topic.

Reyna blinked as her eyes teared up.

"When I got the call about Jimmy, I thought this was it. I thought about how much I depend on him, without even realizing it. He has always been there, even when I didn't want him to be. And now when things have gotten better between us, I thought I was going to lose him."

Now Ms. De Groot turned to Ruiz. "What do you think of what Reyna's just said?"

This was as close as Reyna had gotten to saying she loved him. Something he'd wanted for a long time.

"This is nice to hear, Reyna," Ruiz said. "I'm sad that it took me getting injured for you to tell me these things."

Reyna began crying, and Ms. De Groot handed her the box of tissues.

"I'd like to say something else." Ruiz felt the wound in his side suddenly flare up as he shifted his position on the sofa. He wondered if it would be with him forever. "I've had a lot of time to lay around and think. I thought when we started counseling that we were trying to get back to something, something we lost when the affair happened. But really, we had *nothing* before. What we're doing is building something new. If I look at it that way, I'm hopeful. And it's not about feeling guilt or regret for what anybody did. It's starting something new because we both decided we want to."

On the drive home, Reyna didn't take the turn he expected, to head back toward Santa Clara. She took the route they'd taken after their last counseling session.

"I texted Colin's mom," she said softly as she turned onto El Camino Real. "The boys will be fine if we're a little late tonight."

A streetlight lit up her pretty features as they passed under it.

"That's perfect." Ruiz sighed and leaned back in the Range Rover's comfortable passenger seat. "Because I could use a mojito."

# THANK YOU!

Thank you for reading *A Tree of Poison*. If you enjoyed this book, I hope you'll leave a review or rating on Amazon, Goodreads or the book review site of your choice.

Ratings and reviews have a huge impact on an author's success. I'm incredibly grateful for the time you take to do this.

# ACKNOWLEDGMENTS

This book happened because so many readers said they wanted to hear more about Ruiz, Grasso, and Flores—so thank you all. I hope this book has been satisfying to you.

Thank you to my copy editor and idea person, Honest Magpie, aka Armen Kazarian, for their hard work on this book and their honest critiques. And to the beta readers: Shannon MacRae Bailey, Chris Anderson, Pam Milliken, Kerry Nozicka, and Patrick Andersen.

Thank you to Debbie Cunningham and Chris Anderson, who are the most supportive friend-fans a writer could have.

To the phenomenal organization Sisters in Crime— SinC National, the Guppies group and the NorCal and Coastal Cruisers chapters. I would not be published if it weren't for these groups—you sisters and misters are a storehouse of knowledge and a lot of fun to hang out with.

Thank you to my husband, Pete, for the encouragement and game-playing. We definitely had a difficult 2022, but I'm thankful we could go through it together.

And to my dad, Stan Vierk, for modeling creativity for me and for being my biggest encourager to write and publish. He read my books on his Kindle not just once but multiple times, in case he forgot "who did it." He passed away at the age of eighty-eight while I was editing this book.

*Ein Prosit*, Pops.

# ALSO BY VL KAZARIAN

SILICON VALLEY MURDER

(Detectives Ruiz, Grasso and Flores)

Swift Horses Racing - Silicon Valley Murder, Book 1

Across the Red Sky – Silicon Valley Murder Book 2

THE LAUGHING LOAF BAKERY MYSTERIES

Writing as Victoria Kazarian

Drop Dead Bread - Laughing Loaf Bakery Mystery #1

Bread to Rights - Laughing Loaf Bakery Mystery #2

Trouble You Don't Knead - Laughing Loaf Bakery Mystery #3

Sourdough and Cyanide - Laughing Loaf Bakery Mystery #4

Proof of Death - Laughing Loaf Bakery Mystery #5

Stop, Drop and Rolls: A Laughing Loaf Bakery Short Mystery
(prequel novella)

# ABOUT THE AUTHOR

Victoria Kazarian lives and writes in San Jose, California. A former Silicon Valley marketing professional and high school English teacher, she now writes full time. When she's not writing, she's reading, baking bread, or forcing her children and dog to go on road trips to the Pacific Northwest. You can contact her at vkazarian@gmail.com

# ARE YOU IN A BOOK CLUB?

Are you in a book club?
Interested in reading any of the *Silicon Valley Murder* or *Laughing Loaf Bakery* mysteries? I'd love to appear at your book club virtually - or in person, if you're in the San Francisco Bay Area.
Contact me at thelaughingloaf@gmail.com